DEATH OF YESTERDAY
and M. C. BEATON'S ACCLAIMED MYSTERIES
FEATURING HAMISH MACBETH

"Hamish Macbeth is that most unusual character, one to whom the reader returns because of his charming flaws. May he never get promoted."
—*New York Journal of Books*

"Author M.C. Beaton has produced some of the coziest of cozies over the years... You have so much fun watching Hamish's clueless bungling of every romantic possibility and getting to know the denizens of Lochdubh that 'whodunit' scarcely matters... [Curl] up in your favorite chair, and prepare yourself to enjoy DEATH OF YESTERDAY."
—BookReporter.com

"With residents and a constable so authentic it won't be long before tourists will be seeking Lochdubh and believing in the reality of Hamish Macbeth as surely as they believed in Sherlock Holmes."
—*Denver Rocky Mountain News*

"Macbeth is the sort of character who slyly grows on you."
—*Chicago Sun-Times*

Death of Yesterday

Previous Hamish Macbeth Mysteries by M. C. Beaton

M. C. BEATON

Death of Yesterday

GRAND CENTRAL
PUBLISHING

NEW YORK   BOSTON

Grand Central Publishing
Hachette Book Group
237 Park Avenue
New York, NY 10017
www.HachetteBookGroup.com

Grand Central Publishing is a division of Hachette Book Group, Inc.
The Grand Central Publishing name and logo is a trademark of Hachette Book Group, Inc.

The Hachette Speakers Bureau provides a wide range of authors for speaking events. To find out more, go to www.hachettespeakersbureau.com or call (866) 376-6591.

The publisher is not responsible for websites (or their content) that are not owned by the publisher.

Printed in the United States of America

Originally published in hardcover by Hachette Book Group
First mass market edition: February 2014

10 9 8 7 6 5 4 3 2 1
OPM

*To my good neighbours, Louise Bowles and
Samantha Burke, with affection*

Chapter One

Send home my long stray'd eyes to me,
Which O! too long have dwelt on thee

—William Blake

Morag Merrilea was an art student, earning money in her summer holidays by working as a secretary for Shopmark Fashions in Cnothan in the Scottish county of Sutherland. She was English and considered herself a cut above her fellow workers. She was highly unpopular. Her appearance was unprepossessing. She had lank brown hair and rather prominent green eyes. But she had a passion for art and for studying faces.

Shopmark Fashions was a new factory on the outskirts of the village, risen out of an old derelict Victorian furniture store. Cnothan was a grim place with one main street running down to a man-made loch over which towered the grey walls of a hydroelectric dam.

Morag had taken the job because she had dreamt of a romantic highland village, and had never quite got over the culture shock of being in Cnothan where the sour locals took pride in "keeping themselves to themselves."

She sat in her usual corner of the Highlander pub one Saturday evening with her sketchbook, busily drawing the faces of people in the pub, and also the face of someone looking in at the window. Morag always drank alone. The other employees of the factory drank at a pub down on the lochside and, strangely enough, Morag's solitary drinking was not remarked on because of her unpopularity and the locals shying away from any mention of her.

Although not particularly imaginative, that particular evening she seemed to feel the remoteness, the very foreignness of Sutherland pressing in on her, a claustrophobic sense that the great towering mountains were creeping closer across the heathery moors. The result was, she drank more than usual. The pub was quite full with forestry workers, crofters, and the unemployed. Morag was brilliant at drawing faces and felt the very act of drawing people, of getting them on paper, put them in her power.

At one point, she went to the lavatory. When she returned, she found her sketchbook was missing. She complained to the barman and to everyone around.

Getting nothing in reply but blank stares, she downed her drink and made for the door. Morag collapsed outside and was taken to hospital.

After she came awake the following morning and received a lecture from a young doctor on the evils of drink, Morag was gripped with a sudden fear that she might be an alcoholic. She had drunk four pints of beer and assumed she had experienced a blackout. She could not remember the previous evening at all.

She did have one friend at Hornsey Art College where she had studied. She phoned her friend, Celia Hedron, and told her about losing her memory.

Celia said sharply, "Have you considered that someone might have slipped you a date rape drug? That blacks you out so you can't remember things."

This dramatic solution appealed to Morag, who did not like to think she was a common alcoholic. She dithered for a week before catching a bus from Cnothan and presenting herself at the police station in Lochdubh. She had been told the police sergeant, Hamish Macbeth, was also responsible for policing Cnothan—along with vast tracts of Sutherland.

Her first impression of Hamish Macbeth was a bad one. When she arrived, he was up on a ladder clearing out the guttering. His lazy constable, Dick Fraser, a plump man with a grey moustache, was sleeping peacefully in the front garden on a deck chair.

"You!" shouted Morag. "Get down here immediately. I have a crime to report."

Hamish came slowly down the ladder. She saw a tall man with flaming red hair and hazel eyes.

"What seems to be the problem?" he asked.

Morag threw back her head and declared, "I have been drugged, raped, and my sketchbook has been stolen."

"Then you'd better come ben to the office," said Hamish mildly.

"Whassat?" mumbled Dick and went back to sleep.

Hamish led the way in at the side door, through the kitchen, and into his small office, where he pulled out a chair for her. He wrote down the details of her addresses in Cnothan and London along with her phone numbers at home and work.

"It's like this," said Morag. She gave him her view of what had happened, along with details of her age, twenty-three, and her work as a secretary at the clothes factory.

"And when exactly did this take place?" asked Hamish.

"Last Saturday week."

Hamish had been taking notes. He put down his pen. "If you were drugged with some date rape drug, it would no longer be in your system. Were you checked for signs of rape?"

"Well, no."

"I think we should go to the hospital right away and have you checked."

Morag bit her lip. She had examined herself and knew there were no signs of bruising or forced entry. "I can't be bothered," she said.

"Then I don't see what you expect me to do," said Hamish patiently.

"You are a moron," said Morag. "You could at least make some push to get my sketchbook back—that is if you ever get off your arse and do anything."

"What were you sketching?"

"Faces of people in the pub. Oh, and someone who looked in at the window."

"Are you any good?" asked Hamish bluntly.

She opened her large handbag, pulled out a small sketchpad, and handed it to him.

His interest quickened. She was very good indeed.

"I'll need to take a note of who was in the pub. Can you remember any names?"

"They're all just faces to me—Angus this and Jimmy that. I do not consort with the local peasantry. The factory staff drink at the Loaming down on the loch."

"With an attitude like that," said Hamish, the sudden sibilance of his accent showing he was annoyed, "I'm fair astounded that someone didnae try to bump you off instead of chust slipping something in your drink."

"You're as useless as the rest of..."

"Calm down, lassie. I hae this idea…"

"Wonders will never cease."

"Oh, shut up and listen for once in your life. I know a hypnotist down in Strathbane. He might be able to put you under and restore some o' your memory."

Morag's protruding eyes gleamed. The drama of such a suggestion appealed to her along with the idea of rattling the cage of whoever had drugged her drink.

"I'll make an appointment and let you know," said Hamish.

Hamish wondered as he set off for Strathbane later that day with Dick why he was even bothering to help such an unlovely character as Morag Merrilea. He cursed himself for not having asked exactly how much she had to drink. She could simply have had an alcoholic blackout.

Still, he reminded himself, he wasn't doing anything else at the moment. The summer was unusually warm, with those nasty biting midges of the Highlands out in force. Patel's, the local shop in Lochdubh, had sold out of insect repellant.

As they mounted a crest of the road, Dick said, "Every time I see Strathbane, I'm right glad I'm out of it."

Strathbane was a blot on the beauty of Sutherland. Once a busy fishing port, it had died when the fishing stocks ran out. Drugs arrived and it became a town with an air of dirt and desolation.

"I don't like this idea of a hypnotist," said Dick. "Sounds awfy like black magic."

"Och, even Strathbane police use Mr. Jeffreys from time to time."

"Did they say they would pay his bill?"

Hamish shifted uncomfortably in the driver's seat. He knew that Detective Chief Inspector Blair, the bane of his life, would have put a stop to it.

"It's fine," he said airily. "He'll just send in his bill as usual."

Dick was disappointed in Mr. Jeffreys. He had expected to meet an elderly guru.

But Jeffreys was only in his thirties, a thin man with brown hair in a ponytail, dressed in torn jeans and a T-shirt.

"Let me see," said Jeffreys. "I can fit her in at three o'clock next Saturday."

Hamish phoned Morag on her mobile. She was delighted. "Wait till those bastards in the pub hear about this!"

"I wouldnae go around shooting your mouth off," cautioned Hamish. "I'll collect you on Saturday and take you to Strathbane."

In the three days leading up to Saturday, Hamish and Dick pottered around the police station. To Dick Fraser, it was paradise. Viewed as useless by headquarters in Strathbane, he had been relocated to Lochdubh. He was a quiz addict, appearing on television quiz shows, and the kitchen in the police station gleamed with his winnings—an espresso coffee making machine, a dishwasher, a new washing machine, and a new microwave.

The single and widowed ladies of the village began to regard him as prime husband material, but Dick showed no interest, preferring to dream in a deck chair in the front garden by day and watch television in the evenings.

He was roused from his lethargy on Saturday by Hamish. "We'd better go and pick up yon Morag female," said Hamish. "Get your uniform on."

Morag rented a flat in a Victorian villa on the edge of Cnothan. When Hamish rang her doorbell, there was no reply. Morag's flat was on the top floor. He stood back and looked up. The curtains were open, but there was no sign of anyone moving about.

"Silly cow," he muttered. "I'm sure she wouldnae have forgotten." He rang the landlady's bell.

Mrs. Douglas, the landlady, opened the door. She was a small round woman with thick glasses and an untidy thatch of grey hair.

"Whit now?" she demanded.

"We've come to collect Miss Merrilea," said Hamish patiently. "Is herself at home?"

"Dinnae ken."

"Would you please go and look?"

Grumbling, she shuffled off up the stairs. They waited in the warm sunlight.

At last she reappeared and handed Hamish a postcard. "This was stuck on her door," she said.

Typed neatly on a postcard was: "Gone to London. Will be in touch." It was not signed.

"I don't like this," said Hamish. "Would you mind showing us her flat?"

"Have ye a warrant?"

"No, I haff not!" said Hamish. "But if you don't let me in and show me her flat, I'll come back here with a warrant and I will turn this whole damn place upside down, including your premises."

"Here, now, no need for that," she said, thinking of the cash undeclared to the taxman hidden under her mattress. "I'll get the key."

They followed her into a shadowy hall lit with coloured harlequin diamonds of light from the sun shining through the stained-glass panel on the front door.

Dick eyed the steep stairs. "I'll be waiting for ye outside, sir," he said to Hamish.

"Oh, all right," said Hamish crossly.

He followed Mrs. Douglas as she panted up the stairs. She inserted a key into a door on the top landing. "There's no need for you to wait," said Hamish. "I'll bring you down the key when I've finished."

The flat consisted of a small living room, a cell of a bedroom, a kitchen unit behind a curtain, and a shower. The living room contained a small card table laden with artist's materials and two hard-backed chairs by the window. There was a dingy print of *The Stag at Bay* over the empty fireplace. One battered armchair was beside the fireplace facing a small television set. Planks on bricks along one wall supplied bookshelves.

Hamish went into the bedroom. He opened the wardrobe. A few skirts and blouses hung there and a winter coat. On top of the wardrobe was a large suitcase. He hauled it down and opened it up. It was empty. He put it back and then opened a chest of drawers. There were various surprisingly saucy items of lingerie: thongs and stockings with lace tops.

He sat down on the bed and looked round. She might have had a backpack of some kind to take a few clothes with her. There was no sign of a handbag, passport, or wallet.

He locked up and went downstairs to where Mrs. Douglas was waiting in the hall. "Did she have a car?" he asked, handing over the keys.

"No, she had a bike."

"And where does she keep it?"

"Just outside. But it's no' there."

"When did you last see her?"

"Cannae bring tae mind."

"Think!"

"Oh, I mind now. It was yesterday morning. Herself was just off tae work."

"Was she carrying a suitcase or any sort of luggage?"

"No. She just got on her bike and went off, same as ever."

Hamish felt uneasy. He put the postcard in a forensic bag and went out to join Dick.

"We'd better check where she works," he said. "I've got a bad feeling about this."

At Shopmark Fashions, they found that Morag worked as secretary to the boss, Harry Gilchrist. Mr. Gilchrist kept them waiting ten minutes, which Hamish put down to the usual pompous Scottish boss's way of trying to seem important.

Mr. Gilchrist was a tall, thin man in his forties. He had thick black hair in a widow's peak above a sallow face and wet brown eyes.

"Working on Saturday?" asked Hamish.

"Work never stops," said Gilchrist. "What do the police want with me?"

"Did Morag Merrilea turn up for work yesterday?"

"As a matter of fact, she didn't. I meant to send someone to check on her on Monday if she was still absent."

"She left a postcard on the door of her flat saying she had gone to London."

"Isn't that just typical of staff these days!" raged Gilchrist. "Well, if you come across her, tell her she's fired."

"Did she say anything about going to see a hypnotist?"

"No. A hypnotist? Why?"

Hamish explained about the suspected drugged drink and the missing sketchbook.

"Oh, that? She was complaining about that all over the place. She did drink a fair bit. She was in the habit of making things up."

"Is there anyone she was close to?"

"She kept herself to herself."

Like the whole of bloody Cnothan, thought Hamish.

Dick and Hamish next went to the Highlander pub. Pubs all over Britain had been smartened up with restaurants and pleasant decor, but the Highlander had been unmoved by time. There was one dim room with scarred tables and rickety chairs. The walls were still brown with nicotine from the days before the smoking ban. The only food on offer was in a glass case on the counter: tired-looking sandwiches and a solitary mutton pie.

Hamish recognised the barman and owner, Stolly Maguire. Stolly was polishing a glass with a dirty rag when they approached him. He was a thickset man with a bald head wearing a tank top strained over a beer belly.

Hamish explained they were trying to find out the whereabouts of Morag Merrilea.

"Thon artist?" said Stolly. "Havenae seen her. Usually comes in Saturday evening."

"Two Saturdays ago," said Hamish patiently, "did you notice anyone approaching her table when she went to the toilet?"

"Naw. It was fair busy."

Hamish turned round and surveyed the customers, a mixture of crofters, shepherds, builders, and the unemployed.

"Which one of them was here two Saturdays ago?"

"I cannae mind," said Stolly. "Ask them? I saw her collapsing outside the door and phoned for an ambulance."

So Hamish and Dick went from table to table to receive surly answers to the effect that they had seen her on that Saturday but hadn't noticed anyone taking her sketchbook or putting something in her drink.

But a youth with greasy hair said he had noticed a stranger. "Can you describe him?" asked Hamish. "What is your name?"

"Fergus McQueen."

"Well, Fergus, what did he look like?"

"Hard tae tell. He had wan o' thae baseball caps pulled right down. Small and skinny."

"What was he wearing?"

"Black T-shirt, black jeans."

"The cap. Did it have a logo on it?"

"Naw. It was dark green with an orange stripe."

"Give me your address. We may want you to come to Strathbane and help a police artist make a sketch."

Back at Lochdubh, Hamish sat down at the computer in the police station office and sent over a report. He felt uneasy. It was too much of a coincidence that she should disappear when she had an appointment with the hypnotist.

To his amazement, he got a call from Detective Sergeant Jimmy Anderson later that day. "Blair's decided to look into it," he said.

"Why? I thought he'd delight in shooting the whole thing down," said Hamish.

"I think he feels if there is a crime, then he wants to be the one to solve it. You've stolen his glory too many times."

"I'd better get back to Cnothan and join him."

"He says you're to sit tight and look after your sheep and leave it to the experts."

Hamish groaned. He knew that Blair's blustering, bullying tactics would make the locals clam up even more.

Hamish waited gloomily for the inevitable. Sure enough it came later with an e-mail from Blair telling him it was a wild goose chase and to stop wasting police time and, furthermore, never again try to employ the hypnotist without first getting clearance.

But undeterred, Hamish went back to Cnothan, knocking on doors, questioning one after the other without success.

He was furious when he returned to Lochdubh to receive a phone call from Superintendent Daviot. The locals in Cnothan had complained of police harassment. Blair had found nothing. Hamish was to leave it all alone.

The weather continued to be unusually hot. Three weeks after the disappearance of Morag Merrilea, two men were loading bales of T-shirts onto a lorry outside Shopmark Fashions when they suddenly stopped their work.

"Thon's an awfy smell from that bale," said one, "and it's heavy, too."

"Better cut it open," said his companion. "There's maybe a dead animal inside."

They sliced the twine that held the bale and unrolled it.

The dead and decomposing body of Morag Merrilea rolled out and lay lifeless under the eye of the glaring sun.

Chapter Two

Perhaps some languid summer day,
When drowsy birds sing less and less,
And golden fruit is ripening to excess,
If there's not too much sun nor too much cloud,
And the warm wind is neither still nor loud,
Perhaps my secret I may say,
Or you may guess.

—Christina Rossetti

"You would think," said Hamish Macbeth angrily, "that such a horror would get folks' tongues wagging, but they're all more closemouthed than ever."

Blair had given Dick and Hamish the task of knocking at doors in Cnothan to interrogate the villagers. Tired of looking into blank secretive faces and getting curt nonhelpful replies, they retreated to the café in the main street to console themselves with cups of bad coffee.

"See, it's like this," said Dick. "There was a village here that was supposed to be right friendly but along came the Hydro Electric Board, built the dam and made the loch, and the old village was drowned. So folks say there's a curse on the place."

"Havers!" said Hamish. "They were all rehoused. No one was drowned to come back and haunt the place."

"Aye, but the church was buried in the water. They say when doom is coming, you can hear the old bells."

"My mother remembers the old village," said Hamish, "and she said they were a right lot of bastards. I hate being sidelined."

"Jimmy Anderson will fill you in. I just this minute saw him heading up the main street to the pub."

"Right! Let's go and see if he's got anything."

Jimmy was seated in a corner of the Highlander pub, drinking a double whisky.

"Any luck, Hamish?" he asked.

"What do you think," said Hamish crossly. "I feel like arresting the whole village and charging them with obstructing the police in their enquiries."

"While you're at it, you can charge the whole factory as well," said Jimmy. "Sit down and have a drink."

"I'll get the drinks," said Dick. "Fancy another, sir?"

"That'd be grand."

"What will you be having, Hamish, er...sir?"

"Tomato juice."

"Blair's furious," said Jimmy, his foxy face and bloodshot blue eyes alight with amusement. "'I wouldnae put it past Hamish to murder the lassie himself just tae upset me' is one of his choicest remarks."

"I've got to find a young man called Fergus McQueen," said Hamish. "He saw a youth in the pub the evening Morag's sketchbook was stolen. He lives in a room up on the brae. I called there but got no reply."

"Try his work?"

"He's unemployed."

Dick came back with the drinks. "I think I should go back up there," said Hamish, "and get a look at his room."

"You'll need a search warrant."

"The landlord might let us in. We could aye say that someone told us there was a smell o' gas."

"Wait till I finish this drink," said Jimmy, "and then we may as well go. We've got nothing else."

Up above the village, near where Morag had lived, stood a tall Scottish Georgian building with some of the windows still bricked up, dating from the days when house owners wanted to avoid the window tax.

As they entered the gloomy entrance hall, Jimmy remarked that he bet not much had been done to renovate the old building except to split the large rooms with thin partitions into smaller ones.

Although the day was warm outside, the inside was cold. The landlord was English, a small, wiry man called Jason Clement, who, to their surprise, seemed delighted to show them Fergus's room. "He's a good lad," he said, leading the way upstairs. "Always pays his rent on the nail."

"You can't charge that much," said Hamish, "unless he's working off the books somewhere."

"Don't ask as long as I get paid," said Jason. "Here we are." He unlocked a door on the second landing and flung it open.

It was a very small room with half a window, the other half presumably belonging to the room next door. It was simply furnished with a small table, three chairs, a narrow bed, and a desk. A curtained alcove served as a wardrobe.

"No kitchen or bathroom," commented Hamish.

"My guests use the bathroom on the first floor and the kitchen on the ground floor," said Jason.

"What brought you up from England?" asked Hamish.

"Quality of life."

"What! In Cnothan?"

"It's beautiful round here. I do a bit of fishing. Suits me."

Jimmy drew back the curtain of the "wardrobe." "Clothes are all here," he said, "and a suitcase." He opened the suitcase. "Empty."

Outside, a cloud passed over the sun and Hamish repressed a shiver. "I don't like this, Jimmy," he said. "I think me and Dick ought to stay here and see if he comes back. He's by way of being the only witness we've got."

"Suit yourself." Jimmy's phone rang. He glanced at it. "Blair on the warpath," he said. "I'm not answering it, but I'd better get back down to the factory."

Hamish sat down on a hard chair and looked around the room. It did not look like a young man's room. There was no computer, no posters to brighten the walls. He wished now that he had asked Fergus more about himself. The door opened but it was only Dick, who had opted to stay outside and had become bored.

"I've just thought o' something," said Hamish. "I can't remember seeing any sketchbooks at all in Morag's flat. She might have had a sketch of Fergus."

"Maybe she took them with her when she left," said Dick.

"But she didnae leave," exclaimed Hamish, exasperated.

"We going to sit here all day?" asked Dick.

"If that's what it takes."

Dick sat down opposite Hamish on another hard chair. He closed his eyes, folded his plump hands over his stomach, and fell asleep.

The hours dragged past. A seagull screamed harshly

outside the window. Somewhere a dog barked. Sounds of cooking filtered from downstairs.

"I'll go and interview the other tenants," said Hamish.

Dick gave a gentle snore.

"Useless," muttered Hamish and made his way downstairs to the kitchen.

Three men were seated at the table, eating bacon, eggs, and fried haggis. "I want to ask you about Fergus McQueen," said Hamish, taking out his notebook. "When did you last see him?"

A burly man with thinning grey hair and dazzlingly white dentures said, "Cannae mind. Quiet wee soul. Us three work at the forestry. Fergus just mooches around."

"Hamish!"

Hamish swung round. Jimmy was standing in the doorway. "Come outside. I've got something."

Hamish followed him outside the house. "It's like this," said Jimmy. "Our Fergus has a wee police record. Petty theft. His parents live in Dingwall. He might have gone there."

"Give me the address and I'll get over there," said Hamish.

"No point. Dingwall police have got it covered."

"Jimmy, Morag was aye sketching folk. But I can't remember seeing any sketchbooks in her flat."

"When the murderer put that card on her door," said Jimmy patiently, "it stands to reason he went in and took away anything incriminating. There wasn't a mobile phone or a computer in the place. There's something else. A preliminary examination of the body shows she was strangled with a scarf. Also, she was three months' pregnant. The local doctor finally coughed up, after the usual complaints about patient confidentiality, that she had been consulting him about it."

"That means she was having an affair," said Hamish. "Surely someone knew who the man was?"

"Maybe. But by the time Blair had finished shouting and yelling, I doubt if anyone wanted to confide in him."

"Where is Blair now?"

Jimmy shrugged. "Stormed off, threatening to return in the morning."

"I'm going to ask around the place now he's gone. Is the factory shut up for the evening?"

"There's a late shift."

"I'll get down there,"

"See you tomorrow," said Jimmy.

In his eagerness to find out something—anything—to break the case, Hamish forgot about Dick.

The lights from the factory were reflected in the black waters of the loch. He could hear the clatter of sewing machines. He was somehow surprised that sewing machines were still used, having imagined that some computer technology might have taken over.

It was a small enterprise, he had learned, helped by government funding to bring work to this part of the Highlands. There were eight women busy at the sewing machines while a supervisor walked up and down, checking their work.

Hamish approached her. He guessed she was in her fifties with a pouchy raddled face and piggy eyes.

"No' the polis again!" she shouted above the clattering of the machines.

Hamish gave her a charming smile. "I'm sure these ladies can look after themselves for a bit while we have a dram in the pub."

"Aye, weel, I wouldnae say no."

To Hamish's relief, the pub on the waterfront that the staff used, the Loaming, was fairly quiet. The supervisor, who had introduced herself as Maisie Moffat, asked for a vodka and Red Bull. Hamish got a tonic water for himself and guided her to a table in the corner.

She took a swig of her drink and then said, "I suppose ye want to know about the dead lassie."

"She was pregnant," said Hamish. "Three months. Might you have an idea who the man might be?"

"When herself arrived three months ago, I mind she was stepping out wi' Geordie Fleming. I wouldnae tell that cheil, Blair. Nasty bully. Geordie's a wee meek creature. It waud be the virgin birth if he had anything tae dae wi' it. God, I'm gasping for a fag. Bloody nanny state. Can I have another?"

"Sure," said Hamish. He made his way to the bar, hoping he could get the drinks on expenses.

When he returned to join her, he asked, "Where does Geordie live?"

"Big hoose along on your left called Ben Cruachan. Cannae miss it. Got wan o' thae big monkey puzzle trees outside."

"And what's his job in the factory?"

"He's an accountant. Works in a wee office next to where Morag worked."

"And how long did their relationship last?"

"Och, they went to the films in Strathbane once. Morag was a snotty, nasty piece o' work. Considered herself too good for the rest of us. I think she dumped Geordie after a week."

"Did she have any female friends?"

"Maybe the one. Freda Crichton, works in design. Another snobby bitch."

"Where does she live?"

"Up the main street. Cottage next tae the post office stores."

Geordie Fleming's house was not big. It was a trim bungalow. Hamish looked up at the monkey puzzle tree, wondering if it had been there before the house was built. It must have been, he decided, to grow to such a size.

He pressed the doorbell and waited.

It never really gets dark at night in the far north of Scotland, more a sort of pearly gloaming, when—so the old people still believe—the fairies come out to lead unwary highlanders astray.

The door opened and a young woman stood there, looking up at the tall figure of Hamish. She was a highland beauty. She had a pale white face and brown-gold eyes like peat water. Her thick, black glossy hair fell almost to her waist. She was wearing a thin cambric blouson over brief shorts and low-heeled strapped sandals.

Hamish whipped off his cap. "Is Mr. Fleming at home?"

"My brother is in the shower. What is this about?"

"I am investigating the death of Morag Merrilea."

"You'd better come in."

She led the way into the living room. "Take a seat and I'll tell him you're here."

Hamish looked around. It was such a plain, ordinary-looking room to house such a goddess. There was a three-piece suite in brown cord. A low coffee table held a few fashion magazines. The carpet was brown with swirls of red and yellow. A small television stood on its metal stand in a corner. There were no photographs, books, or paintings. The room was dimly lit with one standard lamp in the corner.

Hamish was about to sit down when she returned. He got to his feet. She surveyed the tall policeman with the hazel eyes and flaming red hair. "Geordie will be with you shortly."

"I haven't introduced myself. I'm Sergeant Hamish Macbeth from Lochdubh."

"I'm Hannah Fleming. I'm up from Glasgow." Her voice had a pleasant lilt. "Do sit down."

Hamish sat down in one of the armchairs, and she perched on the edge of another.

"Are you here on holiday?"

"Just a short visit," said Hannah.

"And what do you do in Glasgow, Miss Fleming. It is 'miss'?"

"Yes. I work as public relations officer for Dollyton Fashions in the arcade in Buchanan Street. Oh, here's Geordie. I'll leave you to it."

Hamish guessed that Geordie Fleming was possibly in his thirties, although his stooped shoulders and thinning black hair made him look older. It was hard to believe he was the brother of such a beauty. He was wearing a dressing gown over his pyjamas and had a pair of battered carpet slippers on his feet.

"I've been interviewed already by your boss," said Geordie crossly. "Is it necessary to go over the whole thing again?"

"I'm afraid so."

Both men sat down. Hamish took out his notebook. "Where were you on the evening of fourteenth July?" he asked.

"Was that the day that Morag said she was drugged?"

"Yes."

"I was probably here. On my own, watching television."

"Do you go to that pub?"

"I don't drink."

"Recovering alcoholic?"

"Of course not! I just don't like the stuff."

"Now," said Hamish, "it has been said that you were dating Morag."

"We went out a couple of times," said Geordie. "Once to the movies and then another time for dinner."

"Did you have a relationship with her?"

"Sex?"

"Well, yes."

"No. She was a patronising cow, if you ask me, and I dumped her after the second date."

"*You* dumped *her*?"

"She yakked on the whole time about what a lot of peasants we were and about how superior she was. Got on my nerves."

"Did you know she was pregnant?"

"No! And believe me, it had nothing to do with me. I didn't even kiss the lassie."

"So who else could she have been involved with?"

"Can't think. You'd best ask Freda Crichton. They were close."

"Would you be prepared to give a DNA sample?"

"Of course. Got nothing to hide."

"Did she say anything about an appointment with a hypnotist?"

"Yakked on about it all over the factory."

"It's getting late," said Hamish, rising to his feet. "I'd better catch Miss Crichton before she goes to bed."

Geordie escorted him out. Hamish looked back, hoping to get a glimpse of Hannah, but there was no sign of her.

"Thon's one big tree," commented Hamish. "Must keep the house dark."

"*Araucaria araucana*," he said bitterly, glaring up at the monkey puzzle. "Yes, it was there when I got the house built. I was going to cut it down but they said it was the lone survivor of old Lord Barrie's estate which got drowned in the new loch. He owned the old village. The bloody thing's got a preservation order on it."

Hamish looked back at the house as he was about to get into the Land Rover. Hannah was looking out of one of the windows. She quickly closed the curtains.

I've had it with women anyway, thought Hamish as he drove off. He had been briefly engaged to Priscilla Halburton-Smythe, daughter of the retired colonel who owned the Tommel Castle Hotel, and then had thoughts of marrying Elspeth Grant, a television presenter, but she was engaged to Barry Dalrymple, the man in charge of the news programmes. He had so far heard no further news of their wedding, which was supposed to take place in Lochdubh.

At first he thought Freda Crichton was not at home. Thinking the doorbell might not be working, he had hammered on the door, but her cottage remained in darkness. He was just about to turn away when a light went on upstairs. He turned back and waited patiently.

At last the door opened and a very small woman stood there. Her hair was wound up in pink rollers above a small nut-brown face. Two small black eyes surveyed him curiously.

"I am sorry to disturb you so late," said Hamish, "but I have a few questions. I am Sergeant Hamish Macbeth."

"I have already been interviewed by the police."

"Just a few more questions," said Hamish stubbornly.

"Oh, come in," she said ungraciously. "But don't take all night about it."

She had a Yorkshire accent.

Her living room was a jumble of swatches of bright cloth. A large table at the window held a drawing board and drawing materials. "Clear a chair and sit down," she ordered.

"I believe you were a friend of Morag's," said Hamish.

"For the umpteenth time—yes."

"How would you describe her?"

"Clever. Intelligent. A good friend."

"Was she having an affair with any of the men at the factory?"

"Absolutely not. She wouldn't lower herself."

"Yet she was three months' pregnant," said Hamish.

She stared at him out of those small black eyes and then she dipped her head and began to cry. Great sobs racked her small body.

"There now," said Hamish. He rose up and went and knelt in front of her and gathered her in his arms. "Shh, now. It'll be all right. Tell Hamish what's bothering you."

He held her and patted her back until the crying ceased. She pulled a handkerchief out of her dressing gown pocket and mopped her eyes.

Hamish retreated to his chair. "She couldn't have been," said Freda finally.

"Well, she was, sure as sure."

"Maybe some bastard drugged her like they did the night she disappeared."

"Morag did not complain," said Hamish quietly. "In fact, she consulted the local doctor to confirm the pregnancy."

"But we were mates. I loved her!" wailed Freda. "She said she loved me. She said we'd be together always."

"Are you by way of being a lesbian?" asked Hamish.

"Yes. So what?"

"So nothing," said Hamish sharply, thinking that

Morag could not have been much of a friend. "I have to ask you what you were doing on the evening of the fourteenth of July."

"I was here, working on some designs."

"And you didn't go to the pub?"

"I didn't even know Morag went there. Why did she go there?"

To sketch the locals and feel superior to them, thought Hamish.

"Did she talk to you about men?"

"No, we had better things to talk about. Someone must have raped her to get her pregnant."

"I'm afraid that can't be the case or she would have reported it. Now, did she tell you that she was to consult a hypnotist?"

"Yes, she was very excited about it. She spent the night with me and then went off that Saturday morning to go to her digs. She said she was going to the factory to work on something."

"Do you have any of her sketches?"

"I did have a lot. But that last time she was here, she said someone was interested in buying them and took them all away. Do you mind leaving now? I've had a bad shock."

"I'll come back when you're feeling better."

Once back in the Land Rover, Hamish phoned Jimmy and reported his conversation with Freda.

"Now, there's a motive at last," said Jimmy. "Thwarted lover. Feels betrayed."

"Do you have to tell Blair she's a lesbian?"

"Sure. That's the whole point. Why?"

"He's going to jump all over her soul, that's why."

"Sorry, Hamish. Too good a motive. Oh, Dick Fraser phoned from Lochdubh. Seems you abandoned him. He had to hitch a lift back to the police station."

Once back at the police station, Hamish locked up his hens for the night, furious with himself for not phoning up someone earlier to do it for him. His wild cat, Sonsie, purred like a steam engine and tried to climb on his lap as he typed out his report. His dog, Lugs, lay across his boots.

He could hear the noise on the television set coming from the living room.

When he had finished his report, he went into the living room and switched off the television.

"You forgot about me," said Dick. "And I've had a fright."

"What frightened you?"

"Angela Brodie, the doctor's wife, called when you were out. She says Olivia and Charles Palfour are back in Braikie."

Charles and Olivia were two teenagers involved in a series of murders. The murders were proved to be the work of a Russian mobster, Andronovitch. But when his body was found in a pool in the Fairy Glen, Hamish felt sure the Palfour brother and sister were somehow responsible.

"Where are they staying?"

"With Mrs. Mallard, her that fostered them."

"I'd better go and see her in the morning. Thon pair are poison. Why are they back here? They had a new life in the States."

"God knows."

Hamish awoke next morning with a feeling of anticipation. Usually the thought of even going anywhere near Cnothan depressed him. But he had a picture of Hannah Fleming in his mind and he was already rehearsing excuses to call on her brother.

He was just leaving Dick to man the police station and look after his pets when the phone rang. It was Blair. Blair was furious that Hamish had elicited such new information.

"You stay where you are the day, laddie," he said. "Water your sheep or whatever it is you teuchters do. There's enough of us over at Cnothan and I don't want you getting underfoot." And without waiting for a reply, Blair rang off.

Hamish whistled to his dog and cat. He called to Dick. "That was yon scunner, Blair. I'm banished from Cnothan. Going out for a walk."

The day was warm and still with a thin haze of cloud covering the sky. The loch was like a mirror. A porpoise suddenly broke the surface, and glassy ripples spread out on either side.

Hamish leaned on the waterfront wall, wondering whether he should go and see Mrs. Mallard and warn her about the Palfreys. But she thought they were angels and he was sure she would not listen to him.

"Murder in the Highlands and here's our policeman doing nothing as usual."

"As usual" came the echo.

Hamish swung round and looked down at the twin sisters, Nessie and Jessie Currie, spinsters of the parish. Their accusing eyes were magnified by thick-lensed rimless glasses. They had finally put off their usual camel-hair coats and were dressed alike in summer dresses of some shiny material, dark blue with knots of scarlet flowers.

"I am thinking," said Hamish, "just like Poirot."

"Pooh," said Nessie.

"Pooh" came the usual echo from her sister.

They moved on, arm in arm, and Hamish resumed his contemplation of the loch.

Sometimes, he had found, if he didn't know what to do, it was better to do nothing. His thoughts turned again to Hannah Fleming. Beauty, he knew, was supposed to be in the eye of the beholder, but tell that to any man on the planet who would rather have a looker on his arm than a warm, intelligent female who might look like the back of a bus.

Still, he supposed, it always turned out that the lookers were for show and the warm, intelligent ones for marrying unless the man was very rich and ruthless and knew he could trade in the first model for a newer one when her looks faded. And here, he thought, as Angela Brodie, the doctor's wife, walked towards him, is the marrying kind. She had wispy hair, a pleasant face, and she was wearing a droopy dress. But she exuded decency, warmth, and comfort. Of course, her cooking was lousy, but a man couldn't have everything, and the doctor was indeed a lucky man.

"Have you been chased out of the murder scene?" asked Angela, who knew Blair of old.

"That's the thing," said Hamish.

She leaned against the wall beside him. "Have you heard from Priscilla?"

"Not a thing."

"And what about Elspeth Grant? Wasn't she all set to get married?"

"Aye, but Mr. Wellington, the minister, says he hasn't heard any more news."

"Blair will mess things up somehow," said Angela. "Just you wait and see. Have you heard those dreadful Palfours are back in Braikie?"

"I'd better go and see them," said Hamish. "But they fair give me the creeps."

Chapter Three

The isles of Greece, the isles of Greece!
Where burning Sappho loved and sung

—Lord Byron

Olivia and Charles Palfour were much as Hamish remembered them, both having fair hair, long thin noses, and flat, grey eyes. Although they were in their late teens, they were dressed in shorts and white shirts, rather like a school uniform. Hamish guessed the choice of dress was to make motherly Mrs. Mallard still think of them as children.

They both gave him a warm welcome. All for Mrs. Mallard's benefit, thought Hamish cynically. They were seated in the garden, drinking iced lemonade.

"I've just got some cakes to bake for the Mothers' Union," said Mrs. Mallard. "I'm sure you and the children have a lot to talk about."

As soon as she had bustled off indoors, Olivia said languidly, "What does the pig want?"

"Nice to hear you sounding like your real self," said Hamish. "What are you doing back here? I thought you were settled in the States. Come to visit the scene of your crime?"

"What crime, wooden top?"

"Andronovitch. That Russian. I'll swear the pair of you stabbed him and put him in the river."

"I'm now studying law," said Olivia. "That's slander."

"And I'll bet my boots it's a slander you wouldn't dare complain about," said Hamish.

"We've done nothing!" shouted Charles suddenly.

"Be quiet!" ordered Olivia. "The fuzz is just leaving. In other words, Hamish, get lost."

"That murder case is not closed," said Hamish. "I'll be watching you."

"Really? Haven't you got another murder to investigate?" Olivia grinned at him.

"When did you get here?" asked Hamish.

"Yesterday. So if you're thinking of pinning that one on us, forget it."

Hamish took his dog and cat up onto the moors above Braikie to give them some exercise. The warmth of the day made him feel sleepy. He lay down in the heather and closed his eyes.

He was just nodding off when his phone rang.

When he answered it, Dick's voice came down the line. "You're to go to Strathbane. Freda Crichton says she won't talk to anyone but you. Superintendent Daviot says you've to report immediately. Blair's furious."

The small figure of Freda Crichton was crouched down on her hard chair when Hamish entered the interview room.

She looked up at Hamish with red-rimmed eyes. "That bully is accusing me of having murdered Morag. He has made several crude sexist remarks. I want a lawyer. Why can't I have a lawyer?"

"It's Scotland, not England," said Hamish. "You can't have a lawyer unless the police let you have one. But I'll see what I can do. Now, before I start the interview, would you like some coffee?"

"Tea, please."

The door opened and Police Constable Annie Williams came in. "Here to take notes," she said.

"Fine. Could you fetch some tea?"

"Never heard of women's lib? Get it yourself."

"Never heard of seniority?" snapped Hamish. "Me, sergeant, you, copper."

He thought Annie was taking liberties because he had once had a one-night stand with her. It might have developed into something had not Hamish found out the day after that Annie was married.

When Annie returned with the tea, and a recording had been set up, Hamish began to ask questions while Annie sat quietly in a corner.

"Look. I am not accusing you of murder," said Hamish gently. "Nor am I interested in your sexual orientation. Sometimes, in order to find out the identity of the murderer, we need to know as much as possible about the character of the murderee. I know you were in love with Morag, but try to detach yourself from your feelings and describe her as a disinterested observer."

"People thought her snobbish," said Freda slowly, her brown hands clasped tightly round a mug of tea. "But it was her way of coping. She had a terrible inferiority complex. As long as she was looking down on someone, it made her feel better about herself."

"Would material things mean a lot to her?" asked Hamish.

"I know she wanted to be rich one day. She talked about it a lot. She said she envied people like pop stars who suddenly found themselves very rich, you know, money without responsibility. Not like landowners who have to worry about crops and taxes and invasions by New Age Travellers and hearty hikers with their dogs and family."

"She didn't have much chance of it working in a highland clothes factory as a secretary," said Hamish. "Was she on the lookout for a rich man?"

"I didn't know she was interested in men," said Freda. "She—she said I was the love of her life."

"Was she acting a part?" asked Hamish. "I mean, it seems as if she was bisexual."

"I don't know." A tear ran down Freda's cheek.

"So she was pregnant. Think! Did she give you any clue as to who the father of the child might be?"

"Not one. There's something. I mind—oh, about a week before she disappeared—there was this tourist came through Cnothan in a Mercedes Smart Car. Morag said, 'I'm going to get one of those and we'll take off to the south of France on holiday.'"

"Might she have been blackmailing somebody?"

"I don't know any more," wailed Freda. "I thought I knew her through and through and now it seems as if I never knew her at all!"

"Did she talk about Geordie Fleming?"

"She said he was a waste of space."

"He says he dumped her."

"I can't believe that. What woman would look at Geordie?"

"But didn't the very fact that she went out with him make you think she might be bisexual?"

"It was before she took up with me. She said she went out with Geordie because she was lonely and then she said it was better off to be lonely than to be bored by Geordie."

"Any other men? What about her boss?"

"Harry Gilchrist? She despised him. Oh, wait a bit. The head of personnel, Pete Eskdale, used to have lunch with her in the office canteen."

"I thought she would have preferred to have lunch with you."

"She said in backwaters like this, people were cruel to lesbians."

"Odd, that," commented Hamish. "I mean, folk would just think you were nothing more than a pair of female employees."

"I don't know anything any more," said Freda and began to sob.

Hamish ended the interview and went outside to where Jimmy was standing.

"So what did you get out of that?" asked Jimmy.

"I think Morag was blackmailing someone," said Hamish, "and for a lot of money, too. I'd like to interview Pete Eskdale. Has anyone else interviewed him?"

"Not as far as I know. Blair's been ordered to take a backseat. I'll probably see you over at the factory."

"Haven't forensics even found just one little clue?" asked Hamish.

"Nothing. Not even one hair or a bit o' spit. But they say she was killed elsewhere and from the marks on her body, she'd been lying on some hard floor. There's good news anyway. We're going to take DNA samples from every man in the factory. If we find the father of that baby, I think we'll find the murderer."

Hamish drove Freda back to Cnothan. She asked to be taken to the factory. "It's better if I lose myself in work," she said. Hamish glanced across at the small, sad, crumpled figure in the passenger seat and felt a surge of hatred for the murdered woman.

At the factory, Freda scurried off. The baling area was taped off, and white-coated figures could be seen searching the whole place.

Hamish walked in the main door of the factory and asked the girl at the reception desk where he could find Pete Eskdale.

"I'll phone him," she said. "I'm Betty McVee, Angus McVee's girl." She was small and plump with a rosy face.

"Is Angus still with the forestry?"

"Aye. Dad's hanging on but a lot are being laid off. I'll get Mr. Eskdale for you."

Hamish did not have to wait long. The glass doors leading to the interior of the factory were suddenly thrust open and a tall, energetic man breezed in. He was in his thirties with close-cropped ginger hair. His eyes were bright blue. His otherwise handsome face was marred by a small, pursed mouth. He was wearing a charcoal-grey suit, a striped shirt, and a blue silk tie.

Hamish looked at him in dawning recognition. "I've seen your face in the papers," he said. "You won the lottery last year."

"Only a million."

"That's surely enough to stop work," said Hamish.

"Not these days. By the time I'd paid off two ex-wives and the children, there wasn't much left. Can we go outside?"

They walked together out into the heat of the day. "Storm's coming," remarked Hamish.

Pete looked up at the cloudless sky. "How can you tell?"

"The swallows are flying low and that means rain coming, and after all this heat, that'll mean a storm. Let's sit in the shade over there on that bench."

When they were seated, Hamish began. "You must have been the one who hired Morag Merrilea. Why get a lassie all the way up from London?"

"It's a new factory. There was a bit on television about new projects succeeding despite the recession. It got shown down south. Morag saw it and wrote and asked for a job. Now, she had a high level of computer skills, and it's hard to get a girl up here with that sort of knowledge. I happened to be going to London on business and I interviewed her and found her suitable. The previous secretary was hopeless."

Hamish took out his notebook. "What is her name?"

"Stacey McIver. Local girl. She's working in Strathbane at an electronics factory."

"I'd better have her address. Did you know that Morag was pregnant?"

"I only just heard. And I know what you're going to ask. No, I didn't have an affair with her. No, I don't know who did."

"As to that," said Hamish, "we'll be taking DNA samples from all the men in the factory."

"I'm afraid that's not possible."

"What! Why?"

"The staff are complaining that it's an infringement of their human rights and so our lawyers have taken the case up with the Court of Human Rights."

"Oh, for heffen's sakes," howled Hamish. "Don't the innocent realise that the quicker we find the murderer, the better?"

"The way they look at it is that their DNA will be on file and they'll be classed as criminals."

"That's not how it works."

"That's the way they see it."

"Morag struck me as highly unlovable," said Hamish. "I'm surprised you hired her."

"Look, I'd have hired a gorilla with her knowledge of spreadsheets and computers. I'm finding it hard to replace her. Anyway, when I interviewed her, she seemed very quiet and modest. It was only when she settled in here that I realised we'd got the bitch from hell. But she was good at her work. Besides, her boss, Gilchrist, never once saw the bad side of her. She could be pretty cunning."

"Often if there's a work affair, it's between the boss and his secretary."

"Gilchrist! He's an elder of the kirk, member of the Rotary Club, and devoted to his wife."

"What is his wife's name?"

"Brenda. Why?"

"I wonder if she ever met Morag."

"I doubt it. Madam considers us factory workers all rather vulgar. She's got expensive tastes."

"I might have a word with her."

"Good luck. She scares the pants off me."

"What about Geordie Fleming?"

"Sad sack. He and Morag were thick at one time and then she went on as if he didn't exist."

"Any other men she dated?"

"Not that I know of. Why did they take poor Freda away for questioning?"

"Because she was Morag's only friend."

Hamish took out his notebook after he had left Pete. For the umpteenth time, he promised himself he would get a smartphone or an iPad. But he had addresses logged in his laptop in the Land Rover as well as in his notebook. He found the Gilchrists' address and made his way there.

The Gilchrists lived in a handsome house on a hill above the town. It was a large Victorian villa surrounded by evergreens.

He rang the doorbell and waited. The day was very still and there was that sort of heavy silence emanating from the house which Hamish knew, from experience, usually meant there was no one at home.

He drove back to Fergus McQueen's lodgings but the landlord, Jason Clement, said he had not seen him.

Hamish phoned Jimmy and asked if Fergus's parents had seen him, but Jimmy said he wasn't often in touch with them. Driving back down the main street, Hamish noticed a few reporters and cameramen wandering up and down. Considering the drama of the finding of the dead body, Hamish thought there might have been more of them, and in the back of his mind was a faint hope that Elspeth Grant might be sent north to cover the murder. Although she was a presenter, because of her background in the area, she had been sent north before to cover stories.

Then he realised that with Geordie at work, he might have a chance to see Hannah on her own.

Was she really as beautiful as he remembered her to be?

The sky above had slowly changed to dark grey, and a whisper of wind caressed his cheek as he got out of the Land Rover.

Hannah Fleming opened the door. Hamish's heart gave a lurch. She really was beautiful.

"What is it?" she asked. "Geordie's at work."

Hamish shuffled his boots. "It's like this," he said awkwardly, "I wondered whether you had heard any gossip about the factory."

"You really need to ask my brother. It's not long since I arrived here."

"But you must have been up here before? Did Geordie introduce you to anyone?"

"Let me see. It was in the spring. He took me round the factory to see if there was anything I wanted to buy. But it's cheap stuff—T-shirts and jeans mostly. They often get coach parties at the factory. The tourists are presented with T-shirts with the logo I LOVE THE HIGHLANDS on them as part of their package deal. How that factory copes with the Chinese competition, I'll never know."

"Did you ever meet Mrs. Gilchrist?" asked Hamish, wishing she would invite him indoors.

"Yes, we were invited for dinner last June. Overbearing woman and a bully. Is there anything else?"

"No." Hamish half turned away. Then he turned back and blurted out, "Will you have dinner with me one evening?"

"Oh, why not? It's pretty boring here. Where?"

"There's a good Italian restaurant in Lochdubh. I could drive you over there this evening."

"Make it tomorrow. I'll drive myself over. Say, eight o'clock."

"Grand."

Hamish sang as he drove to Lochdubh. It seemed such a long time since he had been able to look forward with such anticipation to anything.

Halfway to Lochdubh, the moors were lit up with a great sheet of lightning followed by a crash of thunder. The rain came down in torrents.

When Hamish got to Lochdubh, he stopped on the hunchbacked bridge at the entrance to the village to check the height of the water in the River Anstey. He struggled into his oilskins and got down from the Land Rover and leaned on the parapet of the bridge. The water was racing and foaming underneath, the normally placid river having been turned into a raging torrent. He hoped the rain wouldn't last long or he'd need to get villagers out with sandbags to stop the village being cut off.

And then like something in a horror movie, a body came hurtling down the water. A white dead face with staring eyes looked up at Hamish before the body rolled over and was swept down into the loch.

Cursing, Hamish stripped off his oilskins and uniform down to his underpants and made his way down to the beach. He plunged into the water, swam to where he had seen the body disappear, and then dived.

He dived and dived again without success. He was about to give up when the fast current from the river pouring into the loch sent the body up to the surface again.

Hamish grabbed it and pulled it free of the current and towed it to shore while the heavens above flashed with lightning and roared with thunder as if Thor and all his horsemen were riding the inky skies.

He laid the body on the shingle. It was Fergus McQueen.

As the pathologist went into a hastily erected tent over the body, the sky was paling in the west. Thunder rolled away in the distance.

Dick had turned up with dry clothes for Hamish. They stood side by side under a large golf umbrella. A little way away from them stood Blair. His wife, Mary, did her best to keep him off the booze, but Hamish saw, from one look at the man's truculent and bloated face, that the chief detective inspector had been on one of his binges.

Police had been sent upstream to see if they could find any evidence of where the body had entered the river.

A television crew appeared on the scene. To Blair's fury, the reporter, a small blonde female, went straight to Hamish. "We hear you pulled the body out of the water, Mr. Macbeth. Could you describe what happened?"

Blair lumbered forward and put his bulk between the camera and Hamish. "Macbeth," he snarled, "get back to the station and put in your report, then join the others up the stream."

"Wait a minute." Blair swung round. Superintendent Daviot appeared on the scene. "I see no reason why Macbeth cannot give a brief statement to the press," he said. "Go ahead."

Daviot loved appearing on television. He smoothed back the silver wings of his hair and took his place beside Hamish.

More press arrived in time to hear Hamish's statement while Blair prowled around, trying to conceal his fury.

Daviot then made a statement commending Hamish's resourcefulness and bravery.

Hamish was glad to finally escape back to the police station and to a welcome from his pets. He had just finished his report when Jimmy Anderson arrived. "Got any whisky?" he asked. "I'm fair droochit."

Hamish took down a bottle from the kitchen cupboard. "How was he killed? I assume he didnae just fall in."

"Stabbed in the back. Long, thin sharp instrument. Any idea where the murder might have taken place?"

"A good place to look would be up at the falls. Say the lad met someone up there. There's a wee bridge over the falls. Could have been stabbed and thrown over. I'll get up there, but I should think the rain must have washed any evidence away."

Jimmy tossed back his whisky, shuddered, and said, "I'll come with you."

"I'd better stay here," said Dick, "in case there are any calls."

If Hamish had not been so keen to have someone to look after his beloved pets, he would have ordered the lazy policeman to join them.

By the time Hamish and Jimmy had reached the top of the waterfall, the sky above was clearing rapidly. A late sun shone on rainbows in the spray of the roaring, cascading waterfall. They stood on the small rustic bridge which spanned the top of the waterfall and searched inch by inch.

Nothing.

The bridge seemed to have been scrubbed clean by the deluge. "What a waste of time," grumbled Jimmy. "I could do with a drink. Are you sure there isn't another place we should be looking at?"

"I can't hear you," shouted Hamish above the roar of the water. "Let's get back to the Land Rover."

Out of the sound of the water, Jimmy repeated his question. Hamish looked around the rain-sodden countryside where rainwater glittered and shone on the heather.

"Just suppose," he said, "that Fergus thought he

knew something about the murderer and tried to black-mail him. The murderer would not want to meet him anywhere near Cnothan."

"Depends how long he's been dead," said Jimmy. "He could just have fallen in."

"After being missing all this time? I doubt it. Maybe we should get out again and look further upstream."

"Have you anything to drink in this vehicle of yours?" asked Jimmy.

"I have a flask of brandy for the emergencies."

"Tell you what, laddie, pass it over and go and look yourself. That's an order."

Hamish opened the glove compartment and handed over the flask. He was glad to be on his own and have time to think. He was feeling weary after his plunge into the loch.

He trudged back up the stream. Then he cursed his memory. He had forgotten that a little way up the road from where he had parked was the car park for tourists to leave their vehicles and view the falls. Beside the car park was a recently disused gift shop. There had been some quarrel over the ownership of the shop. Colonel Halburton-Smythe had leased the shop. The lease had run out, and no one else had come forward to take the place of the previous tenants. Local vandals had smashed the windows, and the door was hanging on its hinges.

He went inside. A few roaches left by pot smokers

were lying on the dirty floor. But on a battered table was a half bottle of whisky with a couple of inches still in it and two glasses.

He went outside and phoned Jimmy. "You'd better get SOCO up here. I should have remembered the place. I'm up at the old gift shop. You only have to come a few yards up the brae."

When Jimmy arrived and peered in the door, he said cynically, "I don't think any murderer would have left proof like that. And surely tourists still park here."

"Not at night," said Hamish. "Our murderer may have drugged Fergus and dragged the body to the falls. He was just a wee, thin chap. Put out a bulletin and find out if anyone was up near the falls and saw anything."

They waited a long time. The Scenes of Crimes Operatives did not turn up until an hour later.

The leader, Jock Bruce, asked, "Did you go in there, Hamish? You should ha' known better than to muck up the scene."

"I had to look," said Hamish. "He turned to Jimmy. I'll go back and write up my report."

But as he entered the police station, he found Charles Palfour waiting for him in the kitchen. From the living room came the sound of the television.

"What brings you here?" asked Hamish.

"I thought you could help me," said Charles.

At that moment, the kitchen door opened and Olivia

strode in. "I've been looking for you, dear brother. What are you doing here?"

"I saw the commotion at the bridge and came to ask what it was all about," said Charles.

"I can tell you all about that," said Olivia briskly. "Come along."

Charles got to his feet. Hamish took out one of his cards, and as Charles passed him, he slipped it into his pocket.

"Are you sure you didn't want to say something to me?" said Hamish to Charles's retreating back.

"No, he doesn't," said Olivia.

They went out. Hamish strode into the living room. Dick was ensconced in an armchair with the dog and cat at his feet. Switching off the television, Hamish demanded, "Did Charles say anything to you while he was waiting for me?"

"Not a word. Said he would only talk to you."

"Damn! That boy's about to crack. While you've been lounging here, you lazy sod, I found another body."

Dick settled himself more comfortably in his chair. "Aye, Fergus McQueen."

"You're a policeman. Didn't it cross your mind to go and have a look?"

"I was about to, but just afore Charles arrived, Archie Maclean came by with some fish and told me the place was fair swarming with coppers. I thought I'd just be in the way."

"Well, get along there and see what you can find out. I want to know what time he was killed."

"They won't know that until there are the results of the autopsy," said Dick, reaching for the remote control.

"Out! Now!" shouted Hamish, exasperated.

As he sat down at his desk in the police office to prepare his report, he could hear Dick grumbling to the animals, "Makes me sick. He comes in here all wet and trachalt, so he wants me to go out and get as miserable as he is."

Hamish sighed as he switched on the computer. This second body would bring the press in droves.

Chapter Four

Th' expense of spirit in a waste of shame
Is lust in action

—William Shakespeare

Things in the real world, thought Hamish, the next morning, as he went up the back of the police station to check on his sheep, move so slowly. People had become so accustomed to *CSI* programmes on television that they expected instant forensic results. All he saw before him was a long wait for the results of the autopsy, and more plodding door-to-door asking questions that had probably been asked already by some policeman of the squad that an infuriated Blair was no doubt unleashing on Cnothan and the surrounding countryside.

But his date with Hannah shone in his brain. He knew he should not be dating the sister of a possible murderer, but she could have nothing to do with it.

She had been in Glasgow at the time of Morag's disappearance.

He would not admit to himself that her beauty comfortably dimmed any memories of Priscilla Halburton-Smythe in his mind.

The storm, instead of refreshing the weather, had left a sticky sunny day where midges danced through the air looking for people to bite.

He avoided the press as much as he could, leaving Dick to cope with them. Dick had an enviable, easygoing way with the press. He would talk to them happily without giving away one single fact.

Hamish decided to call on Mrs. Gilchrist. If, by any remote chance, Gilchrist and Morag had been having an affair, she might let something slip. A small, wiry man with a bald head was mowing the lawn. He switched off the mower when he saw Hamish. "Looking for someone?" he asked.

"Is Mrs. Gilchrist at home?"

"Naw. I drove herself to the airport yesterday. She's aye taking the foreign holidays."

"Where has she gone?" asked Hamish.

"Herself said she was going to tour through Europe. Och, I swear herself spends more time away than here. How her man puts up with it is beyond me, so it is."

"I gather you work for the Gilchrists," said Hamish.

"Aye, that's right. I'm Sean Carmichael. I'm by way of being an odd job man."

"Did you know Morag Merrilea?"

"I really only met her the once. I was sent tae Inverness airport to pick the lassie up when she came north. What a wee madam! I tried to have a bit o' a chat but she says, 'You're a driver, aren't you? Shut up and drive.' Could ha' skelped her. Cheeky bitch."

"Did she socialise with the Gilchrists?"

"Naw. Mr. Gilchrist says tae me, he says, 'I like to keep a distance between me and the staff. Get friendly and they take liberties.'"

Hamish made his way towards the factory but did a U-turn when he saw Blair's car parked outside. He went instead to Fergus's lodgings but turned away from there as well when he saw the forensic van outside.

Feeling frustrated, he returned to the police station. It was hard to believe all this was happening in the Highlands with no one having seen a thing. You could be up on the moors and feel alone in the world and maybe decide to sing, and, sure enough, some shepherd the next day or so would comment: "I heard ye singing up the brae. Bit too much o' the hard stuff, hey?"

Cnothan, however, as he knew from bitter experience, was unnaturally secretive.

He sat down at the kitchen table with his notes. Dick was outside in the front garden on a deck chair, fast asleep.

He wondered about Pete Eskdale. He seemed a bit

of a philanderer if all his broken marriages were any proof of that. Morag liked manipulating people. It might have amused her to go to bed with him in London to secure the job.

Hamish put away his notes. He roused Dick, saying, "We're going to Strathbane to interview Gilchrist's former secretary. If she's bitter about getting the sack, she might talk more freely than most of them."

Hamish stopped halfway to Strathbane to let the dog and cat out for a run in the heather. "They spend too much time lounging around with you, Dick," he complained. "They're getting fat."

"That reminds me," said Dick, "I'm hungry. I didn't have much for breakfast. Just the one wee bit o' toast and some fried haggis and bacon."

"We'll get something in Strathbane after we see this girl. She works at an electronics factory and there's only the one in Strathbane—Gerald and Simons."

The factory was the only prosperous-looking building on a run-down industrial estate on the outskirts of the town.

Hamish asked to see Stacey McIver and was told it was her lunch hour and she was in the works canteen. Dick brightened and said quickly, "We'll go and join her."

They followed the receptionist into the factory and up in the lift to the top floor to a well-equipped self-service canteen.

The receptionist introduced them and left. "I'll just be getting us some food," said Dick and moved rapidly towards the counter before Hamish could protest.

Stacey McIver was a small, thin girl with a white spotty face and lank brown hair. She had prominent eyes of an indeterminate colour and a large nose.

Hamish sat down facing her. "I want to ask you about your time at the factory working as secretary to Mr. Gilchrist."

"It wasnae fair, sacking me like that," said Stacey. Her voice held the fluting notes of the Outer Hebrides. "I was good at my job."

"So why did he sack you?"

"He said I was incompetent. But I wasnae! Ask them here. I do good work."

"When exactly did he sack you? Was it long before Morag Merrilea arrived?"

"It was the day after she arrived."

"What! But Pete Eskdale told me he had hired Morag in London because the situation was vacant— or that's the impression he gave me."

"That's the way it happened."

"What is Gilchrist like?"

She frowned. "A bit cold and bossy. Made me work

hard. Wrapped up in that bossy wife of his. Mind you, he gave me a good reference and a goodbye hand-shake."

"How much?"

"Five hundred pounds."

Dick thrust a laden tray in front of Hamish. "I can't eat all that," complained Hamish. "Three mutton pies!"

"And two doggie bags," said Dick triumphantly. "Two of them are for the dog and cat."

Hamish turned his attention back to Stacey. "Didn't that strike you as odd?"

"I was so shocked, I didnae know what to think. My ma said, 'Chust take the money. Thae capitalists are aye weird.' My ma's a Communist. I got this job almost right away and it's a lot better than working for Gilchrist. Look, I've got to get back to work."

Hamish took out his notebook and asked for her name and address. After Stacey had left, he said to Dick, who was eating a mutton pie, peas, and chips with relish, "Let's see Gilchrist again. He's got some explaining to do."

Hamish made the mistake of stopping on the road back to feed the dog and cat and to report to Jimmy Anderson what he had found out and asking if anyone knew where Mrs. Gilchrist was.

"I'm at the factory," said Jimmy. "I'll handle it."

In vain did Hamish protest. It was only occasionally that Jimmy tried to grab the credit for work that Hamish had done, but when he did, there was no moving him.

He drove back to the police station in a bad mood. The sweltering weather did not help his temper.

In the office, he sat down and began to type out a possible scenario where Gilchrist had killed his wife, Morag had found out, and so he had got rid of her as well. But what of Sean Carmichael who had driven Brenda Gilchrist to the airport? He searched the police records and came up with the name of Maisie Moffat's husband. Nothing very serious. One charge of drunk and disorderly and another for shoplifting. But such a man could be bribed. Perhaps he had been in the pub the night Morag had been drugged.

He drove back to Cnothan and went straight to the Highlander pub. But Stolly Maguire said he was tired of being asked questions. He knew Moffat but could not remember if he'd been in the pub that evening.

He went round to the factory and caught Jimmy as he was leaving. "It's no go, Hamish," said Jimmy. "Gilchrist got a call from his Mrs. last night from a hotel in Lyon. I phoned her from his office and she was very much alive and as loudmouthed and bossy as folks say she is and she is travelling on her very own passport, so no doubt there."

"But why was he in such a rush to get rid of Stacey, give her a good reference, and pay her five hundred pounds as well?"

"He says she was no good and he desperately needed an efficient secretary. He says he felt sorry for the girl."

"I don't like it," said Hamish.

"Well, there's damn all we can do about it," said Jimmy crossly. "I'll maybe drop by this evening."

"I can't," said Hamish. "I've got a date."

"Who with?"

"Mind your own business." Hamish was afraid that if Jimmy found out he was dating Hannah, he might protest that it was against the rules to date the sister of a suspect. But the very thought of the evening ahead lightened his mood.

He dressed with special care that evening. For once he was glad that neither Priscilla nor Elspeth was in Lochdubh. In the past, they had often turned up unexpectedly when he was dining with some woman or other.

As he was ready to leave, he said to Dick, "Not a word to anyone about my dinner date."

"Just so you know it will be all over Lochdubh in about one hour," said Dick.

"They won't know who she is," said Hamish hopefully.

"Oh, aye? The drums will be beating, the smoke signals will be going up, and by the time you get to the coffee stage I'm sure folks like the Currie sisters will have found out exactly who she is."

The Italian restaurant was candlelit. "On your own?" asked Willie Lamont, the waiter who was married to the owner's daughter.

"No, I'm dining with someone."

"Who would that be?"

"Someone you don't know."

"Is it Sonja?"

"Who the hell's she?" asked Hamish, looking at his watch.

"A new maid up at the hotel. A real fam fatal."

"Femme fatale," corrected Hamish, who was used to Willie's malapropisms.

The door opened and Hannah came in. Hamish stood up, feeling his heartbeat quicken.

Hannah was wearing a gold-coloured sheath of a dress which clung to her figure. Her thick black hair framed her perfect face. She was carrying a huge handbag. Willie rushed to pull a chair out for her. In the candlelight, Hamish noticed her eyelashes were so thick that they cast shadows on her cheeks.

"I'd try the spaghetti carbonated," said Willie eagerly. "I had some for my supper, miss, and it was grand."

"Go away," ordered Hamish. "We'll call you back when we're ready to order."

"I've never had carbonated spaghetti before," said Hannah.

"I think our Willie means carbonara. You'd think he'd have learned the menu by now."

After some discussion, they agreed to order the same thing: starters of avocado and prawns, followed by osso buco. Hamish also ordered a bottle of Valpolicello.

"Tell me about the case," said Hannah.

"I can't really talk about it," said Hamish awkwardly.

"Meaning my poor brother is still a suspect?"

"Something like that."

"Shame on you, Hamish. Poor Geordie wouldn't hurt a fly."

Willie took their order. When he had left, Hamish said, "Have you come across anyone at all that you think might be capable of murder?"

"Not one," said Hannah. "I think you're wasting our time in Cnothan. I think you should be checking the London end. It's all over the place that Morag was a lesbian and having an affair with Freda Crichton. What if she had some lover in London who learned of the affair and got mad with her and came up here?"

He shook his head. "Any stranger would stand out a mile in that pub. They may not remember exactly who was there on the night she got drugged, but they'd certainly remember a new face—and they would tell me, too, they'd be so anxious to get the heat off the locals. There is one case I can talk to you about, and one that still bothers me."

Hamish told her about the Palfours. As they ate, she listened intently. As he talked, he felt they were enclosed in a little world of candlelight.

He then asked her about her work in Glasgow. As she talked, he barely listened, almost hypnotised by her beauty.

Over glasses of strega and coffee, Hamish said, "You shouldn't be driving. I'll take you home and we'll bring your car over in the morning."

She glanced at him from under those ridiculously long lashes. "I'm sure you can find me a bed for the night at the police station."

"Of course," said Hamish, wondering if she could hear his heartbeats from across the table. "I'll be back in a moment. Just going to the men's room."

In the toilet, he phoned Dick and said urgently, "She's coming back with me. I want you to take Sonsie and Lugs and clear off to the Tommel Castle Hotel for the night. Tell the manager, Mr. Johnson, I'll pay him tomorrow."

Hamish and Hannah walked together through the close, warm night to the police station.

Once inside, Hamish said, "The only spare bed is in the one police cell. I'll take that and give you my bed."

"Don't be silly. We'll both take your bed."

"Fine," said Hamish. "I'll get you some clean towels and let you use the bathroom first."

When Hannah went into the bathroom, Hamish rushed into his bedroom and changed the sheets. Then he sat down on a chair by the bed, almost trembling with anticipation.

He then put off the main light and left a little bedside light burning.

Time passed. She seemed to be taking a very long time.

At last, she appeared, wrapped in a large bath towel. She rushed to the bed and got under the covers.

"I won't be long," said Hamish hoarsely.

In the bathroom, he noticed three boxes on top of the bathroom shelf. Curious, he opened the first one. Two thick false eyelashes like dead spiders lay there. The second box revealed contact lenses; amber with flecks of gold. He felt he shouldn't be searching through her stuff, but opened the third square box. It contained a pair of falsies—plastic breasts. And worse than anything, a tumbler held a dental plate with four front teeth.

He suddenly felt cheated and told himself he was being a fool. Surely all women enhanced their appearance one way or the other.

He undressed, took a shower, and with a towel round his middle he went into the bedroom.

After she fell asleep, he lay awake. He had done the best he could and she seemed satisfied, but it had been an unnerving experience. It was the first time he had bedded a woman who was completely flat-chested. What did it matter what she looked like? he scolded himself. But he had been so carried away by what he had thought her beauty that he had not really listened to her and so he did not know what she was really like.

Before he turned to switch off the light, he noticed a loose tress of black hair lying on the pillow. It had a little knob of glue at the end. A hair extension, thought Hamish miserably.

He rose early in the morning, feeling guilty and miserable. If only he was one of those men who cheerfully had one-night stands and gave the woman the brush-off in the morning without any conscience. He knew he could not do that. But he could play for time.

As he sat in the kitchen drinking coffee, he heard her get up and go into the bathroom. To delay the moment when he would have to see her again, he walked out to the waterfront and stared gloomily at the water. The humidity had lifted, and the air was fresh and cool.

When he returned, she was still in the bathroom. He had another cup of coffee. It was over an hour before she emerged, every bit as beautiful as she had been when Hamish had first seen her. He looked at her with admiration, thinking that she was, indeed, a work of art.

"Oh, coffee!" she said. "I could do with a cup. Are you going to be working all day?"

"Yes, I'd better phone in and get my orders," said Hamish.

"But we can meet up this evening?"

Hamish was just wondering how he could possibly get out of it when Jimmy Anderson strolled in without knocking. He looked at Hannah and demanded, "Who's this?"

Hamish introduced them. Jimmy's face darkened. "A word in private with you, Hamish."

"Come into the office," said Hamish. Jimmy followed him in and slammed the door.

"Just what the hell are you playing at, Hamish?" he demanded. "Thon's the sister of one of our suspects."

"She chust called round," lied Hamish, the strengthening of his highland accent betraying how upset he was.

"Pull the other one," sneered Jimmy. "I was buying some whisky in Patel's and thae Currie sisters thought fit to inform me of your romance. Now, I'll keep it from Blair, but get rid of her and don't go near her again until this case is closed. Get over to Cnothan and knock on doors and see if you can get anyone to talk."

Jimmy had expected an argument but to his surprise all Hamish replied was a meek, "Yes."

"I'll be off then," said Jimmy. "You get back in there and give the lassie her marching orders."

"I've just had a rocket about seeing you," said Hamish to Hannah. "I've been told not to see you again until the case is closed."

Hannah looked dismayed. "But does he need to know?"

"You can't keep anything quiet around here," said Hamish.

"Except murder," said Hannah cynically. "I could have helped you. I'm very good at judging people." She began to tell him several very long and boring stories.

Oh, why didn't I listen to her last night? wondered Hamish. I was so captivated by her beauty, I barely listened to a word she said. He also wondered if this was how women felt the morning after when they realised what a mistake they had made. He felt grubby, petty, and stupid.

He at last interrupted her by saying gently that he had to get over to Cnothan.

"I may have a surprise for you," said Hannah. "I'll bet I can find that murderer for you."

"Don't do anything," said Hamish sharply. "It's dangerous."

"Pooh! Nothing frightens me," said Hannah, with the insouciance of someone who has never faced any danger before.

She gave him a passionate kiss to which he tried his best to respond.

Hannah did not go back to her brother's home. Instead she drove to Braikie. She remembered what Hamish had told her about the Palfours. He had said he was sure the boy wanted to tell him something. If she could get Charles Palfour to talk to her, then that nasty detective would tell Hamish it was all right to see her. Hannah could see herself as Sergeant Macbeth's wife. She would be written about in all the papers as a sort of Watson to Hamish's Sherlock. Hannah was possessed of a narcissistic vanity. She had once overheard her boss saying to someone, "Our Hannah has unplumbed shallows." Hannah had simply thought he had meant *depths* and had made a stupid mistake.

She sang as she drove over the heathery hills to Braikie.

Although the locals referred to Braikie as "the village," thinking it sounded posher than "town," it was a town by highland standards, although not very large.

The appearance of a beautiful woman in Braikie, asking for the Palfours, set gossipy tongues wagging. One would say they had seen her on television, another in a Bond film. Even more imaginative were the ones who watched *CSI* programmes on television and swore she had come over from America because there had always been something suspicious about the Palfours.

So Hannah found it easy to be directed to Mrs. Mallard's home. Mrs. Mallard was out shopping but Olivia answered the door and curtly asked Hannah what she wanted.

"I would like to speak to your brother, Charles," said Hannah.

"Why?"

"I am making enquiries on behalf of Hamish Macbeth," said Hannah importantly.

"Show me your warrant card," snapped Olivia.

Hannah gave the girl what she hoped was a winning smile. "Hamish is very busy at the moment," she said. "He believes that Charles was anxious to talk to him."

"If Macbeth wants to contact my brother, then he may do so, instead of sending some tart to waste my time," said Olivia, and slammed the door.

Hannah sat in her car outside the house. She saw what must be Mrs. Mallard coming home but nothing of any youth that might be Charles. She was stubbornly determined to talk to him. He had to return sometime. But night descended—or the gloaming that passes for night in the Scottish Highlands in summer—and lights went on in the house.

Her eyes began to droop and she fell asleep.

The click of the rear door of her car opening awoke her. The next thing a heavy blow struck her on the head and knocked her unconscious.

"Help me get her in the boot," said Olivia.

"We can't do this," wailed Charles.

"Yes, we can. It's your fault for being such a wimp. She's been asking questions all around the town. We'll take her and her car up to that peat bog and shove the whole lot in."

"You're mad," said Charles.

"You want to spend time in prison? Come on!"

They heaved the unconscious body into the boot of the car and slammed down the lid. Olivia settled herself in the driver's seat with Charles beside her and drove off.

"What if Mrs. Mallard saw us?" said Charles.

"I drugged her cocoa. She'll sleep all night."

Charles felt numb cold with fear. He knew that when this woman was reported missing, then the police would quickly learn she had been searching for him. But Olivia had threatened to kill him if he talked, and he was sure she would do it. He began to contemplate the idea of suicide.

Olivia drove up to the peat bog several miles up on the moors outside the town. "Get out!" she ordered her brother. "The brake isn't on. Help me push."

"But she wasn't dead!" cried Charles.

"She soon will be! Push!"

There was an incline down to the peat bog. They both pushed hard and the car gathered momentum until the front pointed down into the bog and began to sink.

"Right," said Olivia. "Let's go. We'll let ourselves into the house the back way so no one sees us. If they don't have a body, they can't do anything to us."

But the front of the car struck a large rock sunk in the peat bog and stopped sinking.

In the boot, Hannah recovered consciousness.

Shepherd Diarmuid Burns, walking back across the moors with his sheepdog at his heels, heard a faint cry coming from the direction of the peat bog. He saw the car upended and heard cries coming from the boot. He knew if he went up to the car, he might sink in the bog. He took out his mobile and urgently called the emergency services, saying to bring ladders as someone was in the boot of a car in the peat bog. He then shouted to whoever was trapped in the car that help was coming.

Hamish got a message from Strathbane, roused Dick Fraser, jumped in his Land Rover, and set off for Braikie with the siren howling.

Charles Palfour, crouched at the end of his bed, heard the sound of that siren. He knew he should wake his sister. Olivia had taken a sleeping pill. Then the thought of actually being caught and arrested came to him on a wave of relief. He hoped against hope it was all over and he could be free of his sister at last.

When Hamish arrived on the scene, the Braikie fire brigade had put a ladder across the bog and a fireman was cautiously crawling along it to the car. The fireman popped the lid of the boot. On a rise above the peat bog, Hamish saw the white face of Hannah Fleming.

Another ladder was produced. Two ambulances had arrived on the scene. A paramedic crawled along the second ladder, and he and the fireman gently drew Hannah out of the car. Together, the ladders side by side, they carried Hannah to safety.

"What happened, Hannah?" asked Hamish, noticing the dried blood matting her hair.

"I was at the Palfours'," she said. "I was trying to help you." Then she lost consciousness.

Hamish dialled Jimmy. "I'm up at Braikie. Those Palfours have tried to kill Hannah Fleming. They hit her on the head, stuffed her in the boot of her car, and dumped the car in a peat bog. It didn't sink. Send backup fast."

It was a long night. Charles and Olivia Palfour were arrested and charged with the attempted murder of Hannah Fleming.

Then Charles confessed that they had murdered the Russian, Andronovitch, and they were charged with that murder as well.

Olivia said nothing. Her eyes were glazed. Superintendent Daviot said they should wait for the results of a psychiatrist before questioning her further.

Jimmy took Hamish and Dick aside. "Look, Hamish," he said urgently, "you're going to be in trouble. When Hannah's judged fit enough to speak, Blair himself is going to interrogate her and it'll all come out about you having spent the night with her. He'll get you suspended for starters."

Dick slid quietly away. He usually masked his intelligence under a show of lethargy, but now his brain was working overtime. He knew Blair was always looking for an excuse to shut down the police station. It would mean the end of the best job he'd had in his life. He loved his usually lazy days and the comfort of the police station. He phoned up the manager of the Tommel Castle Hotel. "Hamish is in trouble," he said. "I wasnae at the hotel. I spent the night at the police station as usual."

"Why...?"

"Just do it."

Dick headed for Strathbane hospital at the same time as a policeman arrived carrying a large handbag. "It's that Hannah female's bag," said the policeman. "She's been screaming for it."

"I've got orders to see her about something," said Dick. "I'll take it up to her."

"Grand."

Dick seized the handbag and went into the hospital. He easily gained access to the private room where Hannah was lying.

"Oh, my handbag," she cried. "Will the press be here? I must fix my face."

Dick pulled a chair up to the bed and said in a low voice, "You're about to lose Hamish his job. If it gets out that he spent the night with you, he's toast."

"Oh, poor Hamish. I won't say anything. Hold that mirror for me."

"You'd better say you had read that case about the Palfours and decided to have a look at them for yourself—nothing to do with Hamish. Keep him out of it."

"But Hamish and I are sweethearts."

Dick cunningly eyed the make-up repairs going on and all the lipstick, eye shadow, and mascara now spread out over the bed.

"Och, a beauty like you doesn't want to waste your time on a village bobby," he said. "You'll be on telly, a beauty like you. You could be in films. This could be your big break."

This went straight to Hannah's narcissistic soul. Her eyes widened. "You think so?"

"I know so. I mean, look at Hamish. He's aye avoided promotion. He's no' going anywhere up the ladder. You'll be stuck in a police station during the long winters. Nothing to do. Thought o' that?"

"But poor Hamish will be so hurt if I dump him!"

"Not as hurt as he'll be if he loses his job. When Detective Chief Inspector Blair arrives to question you, you're to say that Hamish put you up for the night and slept in a bed in the cell."

The door opened and a doctor and nurse walked in. "What are you doing here, Constable?" the doctor demanded. "The patient must rest."

"Just a wee interview," said Dick. "Does she need an operation?"

"Fortunately not," said the doctor. "Her head must be like iron. But she must have peace and quiet to recover from a concussion. Aren't you supposed to be on guard outside the door?"

"Oh, aye," said Dick, making his retreat.

As Dick left, he glanced back down the corridor and saw the policeman who was supposed to be on guard returning, carrying a cardboard container of coffee.

He only hoped the doctor thought one policeman looked like another.

Hamish wondered what on earth had happened to Dick. But Dick was back in Lochdubh, having hitched a lift, and doing what he did best: manipulating and gossiping about how Hannah had been ruthlessly chasing after Hamish but he had turned her down, being too good a member of the police force to have an affair with the sister of a suspect. Hannah had lured him into having dinner with her by saying she had important information on the murders, which, it turned out, she did not. Then she had said she was too drunk to drive and poor Hamish had to put her up for the night and sleep in the cell. Dick had taken a staff room at the Tommel Castle Hotel, next to the kitchen, and only the manager had seen him come and go. And so, when questioned by Blair, Dick was able to claim that he had been at the police station on the night in question and that nothing had taken place between Hamish and Hannah.

Hamish waited uneasily for the axe to fall. Jimmy called on him that evening. "I don't know what happened," he said, "but Blair is fit to bust. Hannah Fleming says you put her up at the station because she had too much to drink and you had to sleep in the cell. Dick sent over a memo to that effect."

"I would ha' thought Blair would be too busy grilling the Palfours to bother about her," said Hamish.

"Oh, he was so carried away wi' the idea of getting rid of you that it fair went to his head," said Jimmy. "I looked in on the lassie myself. She gave me this note for you."

Hamish gingerly opened the sealed envelope. Hannah had written: "Dear Hamish, I was drunk and made a bad mistake. Please forget all about it and don't tell anyone. Hannah."

Hamish passed the note to Jimmy, who read it and chortled, "You're dumped! Just as well."

"So what about the Palfours?" asked Hamish.

"Charles is singing like a canary. Olivia's got a lawyer and says it was in self-defence."

"Think a jury will go for that?"

"Could do. Andronovitch was responsible for the death of her parents. He was a Russian mobster. Charles is begging to be kept in prison. He's now terrified of his sister. Anyway, it's back to our own murders."

Chapter Five

Rarely do great beauty and great virtue live together.

—Petrarch

A month went past after the arrest of the Palfours. Hamish haunted Cnothan, questioning and questioning, hoping always to find someone who would admit to having seen anything of importance.

He could only be glad that Hannah had left for Glasgow. He felt ashamed of his reaction to her fake appearance and certainly did not want to see her again.

In between his investigations, he often wondered why there had been no news of Elspeth Grant's marriage to her boss, Barry Dalrymple.

He would have been amazed had he known that Elspeth often thought of him.

Elspeth Grant's engagement to Barry had fizzled out. At first, at the height of their romance, it had seemed as if they were soul mates. Then gradually, it began to appear that they had little in common. Elspeth could not help marking the relief on Barry's face when she handed back her engagement ring.

She had a new worry to occupy her thoughts. She had been secure in her job as Strathclyde's main television news presenter. She presented the news at the important slots of the day—the one o'clock news and the six o'clock news. But she felt a rival had cropped up to threaten her position.

Hannah Fleming's beauty had so impressed the television executives that they had hired her to present a children's programme, screened twice weekly at five o'clock in the afternoon.

Her beauty and her lilting highland accent captivated the viewers—and Barry Dalrymple as well.

To Elspeth's dismay, Hannah was suddenly promoted to news presenter, taking over the early-morning and evening slots.

Elspeth was often at war with her own ambition. She often wished she could throw the whole business over and return to her undemanding job as local reporter in Lochdubh. It wasn't only ambition, she thought ruefully, but money. She was earning a top salary and had become used to the comforts that had brought her. She loved her apartment overlooking the Clyde. She enjoyed buying new clothes without looking at the price.

So that when Barry ordered her to go north to do a feature on the murders, her heart sank. Hannah was to take over until her return. In vain did Elspeth protest that the story was dead. There had been no breakthrough in the murders.

She found herself gloomily taking the road to the Highlands complete with crew of researcher, soundman, and cameraman.

Hamish Macbeth had learned of her imminent arrival from the manager of the Tommel Castle Hotel who had taken a booking of the crew.

He was waiting for Elspeth in the car park when she arrived.

Elspeth's heart gave a lurch when she saw him. He looked the same as ever with his flaming red hair, hazel eyes, and tall figure.

For his part, Hamish felt he would never get used to the new Elspeth. The old Elspeth had worn thrift shop clothes and had frizzy hair. The new Elspeth had straightened hair and was expensively dressed.

"The other press have all gone," said Hamish. "What brings you?"

"Wait until I check in," said Elspeth. "We'll have a drink and I'll tell you all about it."

Seated in a corner of the hotel bar half an hour later, Hamish said, "You look worried. What's up?"

So Elspeth told him all about the ambitions of Hannah Fleming, ending by saying, "My boss is fascinated by her."

"Aren't you going to marry him?"

"No. That fell through."

"Why?"

"Mind your own business, Hamish. Now, about these murders. I feel this is all a waste of space unless you have any idea of the identity of the murderer."

"You know what Cnothan's like, Elspeth. It's impossible to get anyone to speak." His face brightened. "Wait a bit. With you being a television star and all, they might talk to you. You could be a great help."

"I'll try. Tell me what you've got so far."

As Hamish talked, Elspeth took notes.

At last she closed her iPad and looked at him with her odd silvery grey eyes. "All I can do is ask a lot of questions and hope someone will tell me something they didn't tell you. I don't want to be up here very long. Did you know Hannah Fleming?"

Hamish looked at her and shifted uncomfortably in his chair. "I took her out for dinner one evening, but she drank a bit too much so I had to give her a bed at the police station."

"But isn't she the sister of a suspect?"

"Yes, but she isn't one herself, having been in Glasgow when it all happened."

"You must have talked to her about the Palfours. Is that why she decided to play detective?"

"Must have been," mumbled Hamish.

"That one seems to take men over everywhere she goes," said Elspeth acidly. "I find her quite dull. But men never seem to look beyond the outward appearance. She'll probably end up someone's trophy wife."

"Is Barry into trophies?"

"Hardly, since he was once engaged to me."

"Your personality is better than any beauty, Elspeth."

"Meaning I'm plain? You certainly know how to turn a nice compliment."

"You know what I mean," roared Hamish, turning almost as red as his hair.

Elspeth stood up. "I'd better get to work."

She marched out and Hamish sadly watched her go.

Elspeth decided to start at the pub where Morag claimed she had been drugged. It was late afternoon, and there were only a few customers. Stolly Maguire, the barman, beamed at her. "Not often we get a celebrity in here," he said. "It's on the house. What'll you have? A wee dram?"

"Nothing for me." Elspeth slid a ten-pound note over the bar. "But have one yourself."

"Very kind. I'll hae one later."

"You look like a very intelligent man," said Elspeth.

"On the night Morag Merrilea claimed she was drugged, can you remember anyone who was in the pub?"

A blank look wiped out the welcome from his face. "The polis have asked and asked, miss. But to tell the truth, I cannae mind anyone in particular. Just the usual crowd."

"But when she went to the toilet, did you see anyone approach her table?"

"Och, you know how tall Sutherland men are. The place was busy and I couldnae see over the heads to see who was doing what."

Elspeth turned her attention to the customers in the bar. She diligently began to question one after the other, but no one claimed to have seen anything.

She was used to people being bowled over by her celebrity, but the customers in the pub actually seemed to resent her. At last she gave up and went outside, checking her notes, and deciding to visit the factory.

To her disappointment, she was told that the boss, Harry Gilchrist, was in London. She checked her notes and asked if the personnel manager was available.

Soon Pete Eskdale was vigorously shaking her hand and saying what an honour it was to meet her. But a cautious look came into his eyes when Elspeth began to question him about the hiring of Morag Merrilea.

"I've told the police all about that," he said. "I had

to check Morag out in London first to see whether she would be suitable. It's all my fault. I should have given Stacey her notice on my return. That's why Mr. Gilchrist felt obliged to give the lassie some sort of payoff."

"Does he have a new secretary?"

"I'm still looking around."

"So what does he do for a secretary in the meantime?"

"We rotate girls from the typing pool."

"Do you still have a typing pool in these computer days?"

"Och, it's just an old-fashioned name that's stuck." He glanced at his watch and affected a stagey look of surprise. "Goodness! Is that the time? Got to rush. Sorry I couldn't be of more help."

Elspeth left the factory and sat down on a bench outside. She had become used to people asking for her autograph, but as she had walked back through the factory, heads were bent and eyes averted from her.

There must be one person in Cnothan who might tell her what was going on. She thought back to her local reporting days and remembered the minister of the Church of Scotland in Cnothan as being an amiable man.

She drove up to the manse and knocked at the door. The minister, John Gordon, answered the door himself and looked at her in surprise. "Is it yourself, Elspeth? Come in."

He was a tall, cadaverous man with thinning grey hair and stooped shoulders. He led the way into his study, a gloomy room lined with old books.

"Have a seat," he said. "Tea?"

"Nothing for me," said Elspeth. "Mr. Gordon, what's going on in Cnothan? No one seems to want to talk to me at that factory. It's like being in Soviet Russia. Are people afraid to talk about the murder?"

"I think it's because of the recession," said Mr. Gordon.

"What's the recession got to do with murder?"

"It's been a sink of unemployment up here. Gilchrist opens the factory and suddenly, it seems, there are jobs for lots of people. So if folks are told not to talk to anyone about the late Morag Merrilea, they won't, for fear of being back on the dole."

"Do you think Gilchrist has something to hide?"

"I shouldn't think so. He's a good member of my church and seems to be a devout man. But the factory is his baby. He doesn't want any adverse publicity."

"Yet the whole business of hiring Morag Merrilea seems odd. The poor secretary she replaced was not told she was losing her job until a day after Morag arrived. She was given a payoff of five hundred pounds."

"Gilchrist is an ambitious man. I gather, from such gossip as I've heard, that the late Morag was super-efficient. He told me he could now go on business trips knowing that everything would be run like clockwork while he was away."

"Did you hear that Morag had been having an affair with Freda Crichton?"

"Never! A lesbian affair?"

"Yes, according to poor Freda. But Morag was pregnant, you heard that?"

"Yes, I did. This place is a den of iniquity. I must call on Freda and bring her to the light."

"I wouldn't do that, Mr. Gordon. She is in a state and someone like you attacking her sexuality as something abnormal might tip her over the edge. She needs kindness and support. Is she a member of your congregation?"

"No, but..."

"Then leave her alone," said Elspeth sharply.

"Don't you find her...er...orientation abnormal?"

"I don't. She has all my sympathy. She was very deeply in love and I think the wretched Morag manipulated her to satisfy her own vanity."

"Well, I must take your advice because it is something I know nothing about. Besides, I believe Freda to be a Roman Catholic. Maybe that explains it."

"I don't see what it has to do with it."

"The Catholic Church seems to be riddled with sexual abuse these days."

Elspeth repressed a sigh. She remembered a friend

from Glasgow travelling up with her to Sutherland and saying cynically, "Set your watch back one hundred years."

"Can you think of anyone who might commit murder?"

"I think you will find," said the minister, "that it was someone from her past, maybe someone from London."

Elspeth left the manse and was about to get into the car she had borrowed from the hotel when she was approached by a small, grubby little girl.

"Are you yon lady from the telly?" the child asked.

"Yes. What's your name?"

"Abbie Box. I've got something to sell."

How old was she? wondered Elspeth. Maybe about ten years. Abbie had an untidy shock of ginger hair over a freckled, pinched little face. Her eyes were pale green. She was wearing tracksuit bottoms, rolled up, and a grimy T-shirt.

"Is it raffle tickets?" asked Elspeth.

"Naw. Pictures like that dead woman drew."

"Where did you find them?"

"Up at the council dump. I go there a lot. Sometimes there's good pickings."

"I'd like to see them."

"How much?"

"I'll tell you when I see them. Where are they?"

"Up at the caravan park," said Abbie. "But if my brother is there, you're not to say a word."

"I promise. Get in the car and I'll take you there."

In the caravan park, Abbie directed Elspeth to a dingy caravan up on bricks. "Where's your mother?" asked Elspeth.

"Ma's doing time."

"And your father?"

"Don't know. Never knew him. Wait here."

Elspeth waited impatiently while the child went into the caravan. When Abbie returned, she was carrying a sketchbook. It was stained with water and kitchen refuse on the outside, but inside were cleverly drawn faces, and one seemed to leap off the page: Pete Eskdale.

"You cannae take it unless you pay up," said Abbie.

"I should really take this to the police," said Elspeth.

"Then I'll burn it."

"No, don't do that. How much?"

"Cost you fifty pounds."

Elspeth passed over the money and thought rapidly. "Look, Abbie, if anyone knows you have found this, you could be in danger."

"My brother mustn't know! He'd beat the crap out o' me!"

"Then it'll be our secret. I'll drive you up to the dump and you show me where you found it. Didn't the man or men who are in charge of the dump try to stop you?"

"Naw, I go up at night. There's a hole in the fence."

"Look, forget about the dump. I'll say it was left on the bonnet of my car. Right?"

"Grand."

"And remember! Not a word to anyone."

Elspeth phoned Hamish and said she was heading for Lochdubh with some exciting news. Then she phoned her crew and asked them to meet her at the police station.

Seated at the kitchen table in the police station half an hour later, Elspeth handed Hamish the sketchbook.

"Where on earth did you find this?" asked Hamish.

"It was left on the windscreen of my car."

Hamish studied the sketches and let out a low whistle. "Well, there's Pete Eskdale for starters," he said. "And there's Stolly Maguire behind the bar." He turned the pages over. "Morag said something about a face at the window, but there's nothing here. I'll need to question everyone in this sketchbook. Damn!"

"Damn, what?" asked Elspeth.

"This could have been drawn on any evening. Anyway, I'll phone Jimmy and we'll start with Pete."

"Wait a minute," said Elspeth. "Don't forget. This is my news story. Before you take that book away, I want film of it."

"Hurry up," urged Hamish. "But film it away from the police station and I'll say you did the commentary before you came to me."

Fortunately for Hamish, Blair was away "sick," which usually meant another crashing hangover, and so he was allowed to be at the interview of Pete Eskdale.

"I can't remember when that was," said Pete. "I hardly ever go there and it certainly wasn't on the evening Morag said she was drugged."

"We'll be asking everyone whose sketch is on this book," said Jimmy.

Pete grinned cockily. "Ask away."

Hamish and Jimmy questioned him for two hours but always got the same replies. He seemed supremely confident.

Wayne Box arrived back at the caravan that evening to find it cold and empty. Usually his little sister had a meal ready for him.

"I'll give that brat a right thrashing when she gets back," he muttered. Then he saw a note lying on top of the cooker. It read: "Gone to Gran in Glasgow. Try and get me back and I'll pit the social onto ye. Abbie."

Wayne clenched his big fists in a fury. He had become used to using little Abbie as a sort of house slave.

On the following day, while a squad of police along with Jimmy, Hamish, and Dick descended on Cnothan to question all who had been sketched by Morag, Abbie sat in her grandmother's tenement flat in Glasgow, eating currant buns and drinking tea.

Her grandmother, Mrs. Sheena Box, was a widow in her fifties. She was a thickset woman with dyed blonde hair and a pugnacious face. She worked shifts in a supermarket.

"It's a fair wonder I was at home, this being my day off. How come they let a wee lassie like you travel alone on the bus?"

"I asked a wumman in Inverness to buy a ticket for me, saying it was for my mither. Then I got on the bus wi' another wumman and sat next to her and began to talk as if I was with her. You won't send me back?"

"No, petal. You're wi' me now. I'll get you fixed up wi' the local school. Will Wayne try to get you back?"

"Telt him if he tried I'd get the social onto him."

"Grand. Have another bun."

By the end of another day, Hamish felt he could weep with frustration. Three of the more sober locals, frightened for once into being cooperative, said that the sketches must have been done the Saturday before Morag claimed she was drugged, one saying he was wearing his new jacket for the first time as shown in the sketch, and he hadn't worn it to the pub after that, his wife complaining it was too good to go boozing in. The other two confirmed the date.

Stolly Maguire, the bartender, also said it couldn't have been on the fatal Saturday because he hadn't been wearing that T-shirt.

Hamish found it hard to believe he was back to square one. He wondered whether Elspeth had lied about finding the sketchbook on her car. But when he called at the Tommel Castle Hotel, it was to find she had checked out.

Elspeth had earlier received a frantic phone call from Barry Dalrymple. "You better get back here. We've got to let Hannah go.

"She's making mistakes all over the place. She was talking about a riot in Syria and describing that many had been killed and the silly bitch *smiled* at the camera. And there's worse. She did a report about a wee lassie in Irvine who was swept to her death by a freak wave. It was the last item, so she grins into the lens and says, 'And the moral of that is, be careful where you walk.'"

Hannah was gloomily clearing out her desk when Elspeth arrived back at the television studios. She could not believe this was happening to her. She had been riding so high, signing autographs every time she left the building. She also could not believe it had been because of her performance. She knew that Elspeth had been engaged to Barry and was sure she had dripped poison in his ear. A security man came up to her and said sympathetically, "Need any help with your stuff?"

"That's kind of you," said Hannah. "I can't believe this is happening to me. I'm sure Elspeth is behind it."

"She wouldn't do a thing like that. Maybe she'll get married and they'll have you back. There's a rumour going around that she's sweet on that copper up in Lochdubh."

"I'll be back in a moment," said Hannah. "I'd better say goodbye to Elspeth."

Elspeth looked up, startled, as Hannah approached her with an outstretched hand. "I just came to say goodbye," said Hannah. "Did you enjoy your time up north?"

"Yes, thank you."

"When you're speaking to Hamish, do tell him I enjoyed our night together. A very passionate man."

"I will," said Elspeth. "Goodbye. I've a lot to do."

Hamish fretted as the days passed into weeks and the investigation into the murders was being wound down.

The lazy sunny days seemed to be over. Squalls of wind blew in from the Atlantic bringing rain to pockmark the loch. Low clouds raced across the sky.

Someone in Cnothan must know something, Hamish fretted. Although he liked Dick, he sometimes chafed at his own bachelor existence. He should have proposed to Elspeth Grant a long time ago.

One morning, he walked with the dog and cat to the cliffs at the end of the sea loch and sat on the edge of the cliff, watching the green-grey waves rolling in to crash against the rocks below. Restless seagulls screamed and swooped overhead, and little puffins popped in and out of their burrows.

He found it strange that there had not been one bit of forensic evidence. The bottle and glasses up by the falls had been wiped clean. The whisky had been Bells, on sale everywhere in the Highlands.

Then he thought that maybe now the pressure was off the residents of Cnothan, someone might decide to talk.

As he rose to his feet, he decided to begin at the beginning, as if the case were new. He would go over the ground again.

When he returned to the police station and told Dick his plans, Dick groaned and said, "I hate Cnothan."

"I can't just leave it!" said Hamish.

There was a knock at the kitchen door. Hamish opened it and felt his very soul cringe with embarrassment. Hannah Fleming stood there, beautiful as ever.

She smiled at him. "Aren't you going to invite me in?"

"I was chust on my way out," said Hamish. "Oh, I can give you a few minutes."

Hannah seated herself at the kitchen table. She looked around the well-appointed kitchen with approval. She had come back to the idea of being Hamish's wife. Her sacking by Barry Dalrymple had seriously dented her amour propre. She had found a job as a public relations officer for a cosmetics firm in Glasgow but was not due to start work for a few weeks. But the idea of being married and not having to work again had begun to appeal to her.

"What can I do for you?" asked Hamish stiffly.

"Oh, Hamish! After all we've been to each other."

"Hannah, you gave me a note telling me to forget about it."

"I was being noble. I was frightened you would lose your job."

"And I could still lose my job," said Hamish. "Let's chust forget it."

"We could make it all respectable," said Hannah. "What if we got married?"

Now, the average highlander is capable of telling a great whopping lie, especially when cornered. "I cannae do that," said Hamish. "I'm thinking of marrying Elspeth Grant."

Her face hardened. "You mean she doesn't mind you playing around?"

"What do you mean?"

"I told her about our night together."

"You what!"

"Well, how was I to know you were an item?"

Hamish clutched his red hair. "Lassie, you'll be the ruin of me. Please go away and forget you ever saw me."

Hannah rose to her feet. "I'll leave you to think it over," she said. "It's either marriage to me or I'll tell your bosses."

She tripped out the door and left Hamish staring after her.

Dick emerged from the living room. "I heard all that," he said. "You'll just need to stick to yer guns and say the lassie's lying."

"Blair'll believe her," said Hamish. "God, I wish she were dead!"

"Wish who was dead?" asked a voice from the open kitchen door.

Nessie Currie stood there.

"No one," said Hamish. "What do you want?"

"Our rubbish bin has been knocked over," said Nessie. "It's those schoolchildren."

"It's the wind," said Hamish. "Bins have been sent flying all over the village."

"You're as lazy as ever," said Nessie. "I've a good mind to report..."

"I'll look into it," said Hamish quickly, anxious to get rid of her.

"See you do."

*   *   *

Later that morning, Hannah sat in her brother's office at the factory. She had not told him about her night with Hamish. Apart from Elspeth, she had not told anyone. She decided she never would. Her vanity demanded that it should look as if Hamish Macbeth had fallen for her, rather than being blackmailed into marriage.

"What about us having lunch together?" she asked.

Geordie miserably shuffled the papers on his desk. "Can't. I've got too much work. Whatever Morag was, she was damn efficient. The new secretary is no good and it means more work for me."

"Does the pretty lady want lunch?" asked a voice from the doorway.

Pete Eskdale stood there. "All right," said Hannah. "Where?"

"What about the Tommel Castle Hotel?"

Hannah's eyes gleamed. "Grand."

As Pete drove Hannah up to the hotel in his red Jaguar, Hannah began to wonder if she might not be throwing herself away on a mere police sergeant. She remembered that Pete had won the lottery. Over an excellent lunch and a bottle of wine, Pete talked about how well the factory was doing.

"So the murders haven't affected business," said Hannah.

"No, not a bit. In fact, they've brought more tourists

for their guided tours. And Freda's new designs are selling like hotcakes."

"Tell me about your new job."

Hannah did at length until Pete's eyes started to glaze over. She could feel his earlier interest in her slipping away and so she said, "Aren't you worried a murderer is still at large?"

"Sometimes. But we've been so busy. Och, it was probably some maniac from Morag's past. The police think that Fergus fellow tried a bit of blackmail. I'd better be getting back."

"Aren't we going to have coffee?"

"Sorry, got to rush."

Pete signalled for the bill.

"Pity," said Hannah. "I know who the murderer is. And it's someone from the factory."

"What? Who?"

Hannah smiled. "Wouldn't you just like to know? I'm going to arrange a press conference in Strathbane."

"You're lying!"

"You'll see. You look a bit white. Have I worried you?"

"You should be worried about yourself," said Pete viciously.

He dropped her off at her brother's home and went back to the factory. Pete bumped into the supervisor Maisie Moffat. "Pooh, you reek o' booze," she said, wrinkling her nose. "You've been out wi' Geordie's sister, haven't you?"

"I think that one's off her head," said Pete. "She says she knows who committed the murders and it's someone in the factory."

"So why doesn't she tell the police?"

"Says she's off to Strathbane in the morning to call a press conference."

"I bet that one never gets there."

"Why?" jeered Pete. "Think she'll be murdered?"

"Naw. She made it up."

But the news of Hannah's discovery spread round the factory.

Hamish had not gone to Cnothan that day, as he had to go off with Dick to investigate a burglary at a tiny village up on the west coast called Sannda-said.

The squally wind had died, and as he drove down the heathery one-track road into the village, he realised again how much he loved Sutherland.

The village consisted of only a few houses facing a curved bay of pure white sand. It was sheltered by the soaring mountains rearing up behind it. The house they were looking for was two old fisherman's cottages knocked into one.

Hamish knocked at the door, which was answered by an elderly lady. Her hair was snow white and her face crisscrossed with wrinkles. She was leaning on two sticks.

"Mrs. Macgregor?" asked Hamish. "We've come about the burglary."

"About time. Come ben."

They walked into a low parlour. "When did this happen?" asked Hamish.

"It must have been when I was asleep during the night," she said, with the slow speech of a person who normally spoke Gaelic.

"Do you know how they got in?"

She shook her head.

"Do you lock your doors and windows at night?"

"I've never bothered afore. Please to take a seat."

Hamish removed his cap and sat down on a high backed Orkney chair. A peat fire smouldered in the hearth. An old clock ticked sonorously on the mantel. The stone-flagged floor was covered in brightly hooked rugs. A black cat rose from a rug before the fire, stretched and yawned, and indolently strolled out.

Mrs. Macgregor watched the cat go. "A fine watchdog thon one turned out to be," she said. "We get the odd stranger in the summer calling at the door for directions and she hisses like anything."

"Right!" Hamish put his cap on an old wooden table by the window and took out his notebook. "What was taken?"

"Two silver candlesticks, a silver teapot, two old silver snuffboxes, some miniatures that has been in my family for, oh, over two hundred years. Let me think, some spare cash in a tin in the kitchen, a walking stick with a silver knob, and two wally dugs." By wally dugs she meant those china spaniel dogs which ornament many a Scottish home. The old ones are valuable.

"Are you insured?"

She shook her head sadly. "I never saw the need."

"Who calls on you?"

"My great-niece Bertha Sutherland comes by most days. Oh, and Mrs. Moxton cleans for me because I'm not that fit any more. She does for me twice a week."

"May I have their addresses?"

"You don't think...?"

"No, no," said Hamish soothingly. "But they might have seen or heard something."

"Bertha's got the wee cottage, three on your left as you go out the door. Mrs. Moxton's house is upon the brae behind me. It's painted blue."

"With your permission, I'll take a look around."

Hamish and Dick searched the small cottage, but there was no sign of a break-in.

"I'll be back in a while," said Hamish. "I'll just be asking around."

"What do you think?" said Dick when they were outside. "Poor auld soul."

"We'll try the niece first."

*   *   *

At Bertha's cottage, the door was standing open. Hamish called but there was no answer. "I think I'll just go in," he said to Dick. "You wait outside and give me a shout if you see anyone coming."

"That's trespass," said Dick.

"Och, I can say what with the burglary, I thought something nasty might have happened to her."

Hamish walked into the low cottage. In the parlour were the remains of breakfast on a table. He checked all the rooms, looking under the bed and gently sliding open drawers. He then walked out to the back of the cottage where there was a vegetable bed. Propped against the kitchen door was a spade. He noticed there was fresh earth on it. He picked up the spade and wandered through the rows of vegetables. He found a freshly dug patch at the very end of the garden and began to dig. He had only dug a little way when his spade hit something. He put on latex gloves, crouched down, and scraped away the earth with his fingers to reveal a canvas duffel bag. He lifted it out and opened it. The sun sent slivers of light dancing on silver.

Hamish sat back on his heels, feeling suddenly sad. He felt it would have been better if the burglar had turned out to be some stranger.

He went back through the house to join Dick. "Found the stuff buried in the garden," he said. "What a nasty thing to happen in a paradise like this."

"If I'm no' mistaken," said Dick, "here comes Bertha."

A small woman wearing a tweed coat despite the warmth of the day came hurrying towards them.

"Get those beasts of mine in the front seat," said Hamish. "We'll need to take her in."

"What is it?" asked Bertha. She was in her thirties but her face had a worn look.

"I am arresting you for the theft of items belonging to your great-aunt," said Hamish. He cautioned her as she screeched protests.

He locked her in the back of the Land Rover which was parked outside Mrs. Macgregor's cottage. He took out a camera and went back to the garden and photographed the bag in the hole before lifting it out.

He dumped it in the front of the Land Rover where Dick was feeling crushed with the dog and cat.

Mrs. Macgregor came out. Wails of, "Ochone! Ochone!" were coming from the back of the Land Rover.

"I'm afraid the culprit is your great-niece," said Hamish. "She buried the items in her garden. We are taking her to police headquarters and..."

"No, that won't do. I'm not making a charge."

"What!"

"If you charge her I'll say I gave her the stuff."

"I haff the good mind to charge you with wasting police time."

"An auld woman like me? I forget things these days. I probably gave them to her and forgot."

Hamish looked around the tranquillity of the little village, at the great glassy waves curling onto the perfect white beach. He sighed. He unlocked the back of the Land Rover and helped Bertha out. She flew to Mrs. Macgregor, babbling, "I'm sorry."

"Could ye not have waited until I was dead?" asked Mrs. Macgregor sadly. "Come ben and we'll have a cup o' tea and a chat."

Hamish took out the bag of stolen goods and put it inside the door of Mrs. Macgregor's cottage.

Dick got down from the Land Rover followed by the dog and cat. The animals raced off to the beach.

He told Dick what had happened. "She cannae dae that!" said Dick. "Dragging us all the way up here."

"I don't think it will happen again," said Hamish. "I'll bet Bertha is the only family she's got."

"Curtains have been twitching all over the place," said Dick. "I'm hungry. There's a wee store down there round the bend. I saw it as we came in."

Soon they were sitting on the beach eating chicken sandwiches, which had been made up for them in the store. "Beautiful here," said Dick dreamily.

"It's grand now," said Hamish, "but you never know what goes on in these remote places in the winter."

His mobile phone rang. It was Jimmy. "How did it go?"

"Nonstarter," said Hamish. "I'll send in a report when I get back."

"You'd better get back fast. Hannah Fleming is missing."

Chapter Six

The highest form of vanity is love of fame.

—George Santayana

Hannah, heavily disguised, had checked into a small hotel on the Ness Bank in Inverness. The minute that Pete told everyone she knew the identity of the murderer, the police would be calling on her. But, she decided, if she hid out for a few days and then called a press conference, her picture would be back on television and in all the papers. That tide of fame, which had ebbed leaving her stranded on the bleak shores of mediocrity, would come roaring back.

The fact that she would need to make up something to justify her dramatic statement caused her some worry. But not much. She was sure she would think of something as soon as the cameras were focussed on her again.

She was confident that her disguise of full red wig

and sunglasses made her anonymous, not realising that wearing a flaming red wig and dark glasses in Inverness on a sunless day would get her some curious looks.

And so it was that Freda Crichton on a day off down in Inverness to do some shopping noticed the woman with the red hair in a café. Freda sipped her coffee and studied her. And then she noticed on the woman's slim fingers were two rings, a large amethyst set in gold and a cairngorm set in silver. Hannah wore rings like that, she thought with quickening interest.

If it were Hannah, what was she doing in disguise? The more Freda studied the woman, the more she became convinced it was Hannah. Silly Hannah, she thought. Shooting off her mouth like that to show off. There could be no other reason. If Hannah really knew the identity of the murderer, then she would have gone to the police.

When Hannah got up to leave, Freda followed her at a discreet distance until she saw her turn in at the doors of the Farm Hotel. Self-absorbed as ever, Hannah had not noticed her.

When she reported for work the next day, she told the staff what she had seen. "Geordie's out looking for her," said Pete. "I'd better phone him."

"Let her make a fool of herself for a bit longer," said Freda. "I'll tell the police this evening."

*　　*　　*

Dick was watching television that evening when he called to Hamish who was working in the kitchen, "Come quick and see this."

A presenter for Strathbane Television was saying, "Hannah Fleming who has been missing has just contacted us. She is to hold a press conference at the Red Hackle hotel in Strathbane at ten tomorrow morning when she says she will reveal the identity of the murderer of Morag Merrilea and Fergus McQueen."

"And I'll be right there to arrest her before she opens her mouth," said Hamish. "What is she playing at?"

Jimmy phoned Hamish early the next morning. "Thon Freda Crichton's been on the phone. She's sure she saw Hannah Fleming going in to the Farm Hotel in Inverness, heavily disguised."

"I'll get down there now," said Hamish.

"Inverness police are covering it. Just wait there."

"I'm coming to that press conference of hers," said Hamish.

Hannah, restored to her former beauty, got into her car outside a different hotel that she had taken the precaution of checking into the night before. It would not start.

She had phoned her brother the night before, her never usually active conscience working for once and prompting her to allay his fears. Hannah warned him, however, not to tell the police where she was.

She was about to go into the hotel to call for a taxi when a Range Rover drove up and a voice said, "Hannah! Everyone's looking for you."

"My car won't start," said Hannah desperately. "I've got to get to Strathbane."

"I'm going there myself. Hop in."

The conference room at the Red Hackle hotel was crammed with press and police. Ten o'clock came and went and there was no sign of Hannah. Her brother was there, having seen the news of his missing sister on television the night before, but he had not given the police the name of her new hotel.

By ten thirty, some of the press were beginning to drift towards the bar, saying it was nothing but a hoax.

Jimmy said furiously to Hamish, "There's been a right cock-up. The police in Inverness say she wasn't at the hotel. They're searching the other hotels."

His phone rang. He walked off a little way to answer it. When he had finished his call, he came back to Hamish. "She'd moved to a hotel on the outskirts, but by the time they got there, she had gone."

"Anything on CCTV?"

"They're looking. Her car's outside."

"She was using her own car?"

"Aye, but they only started searching last night."

"Come on, Dick," said Hamish.

"Where are you going?" asked Jimmy.

"I'm going to check the road between here and Inverness."

It was a steel-grey day, weeping drizzle. The mountains were hidden, and all colour seemed to have been bleached from the sodden landscape.

"Why are you taking the Struie Pass?" asked Dick.

"If I wanted to dump a body, that's the route I would take," said Hamish. "Practically everyone uses the new road now."

"Do you think she's dead?" asked Dick.

"I cannae think of any other reason why the lassie wouldn't turn up."

"Could be anywhere," said Dick gloomily.

"We've got to try. Keep looking."

The Land Rover moved slowly up the twisting one-track road. They stopped from time to time. Hamish scanned the surrounding landscape with binoculars.

The day dragged on as they slowly approached the viewpoint. Hamish's phone rang. It was Jimmy.

"You're never going to believe this. The CCTV cameras outside the hotel and inside weren't working. The guests were at breakfast, which is in the dining room at the back. No one saw her leave. What are you doing?"

"Still searching," said Hamish gloomily.

"If she's been hijacked, then whoever took her is right bold," said Jimmy. "To take her off in broad daylight!"

"Someone was desperate," said Hamish. "I'll phone you as soon as I get anything."

"We've got men over at the factory taking statements, finding out where everyone was this morning."

"Pete Eskdale?"

"Over in Strathbane, drumming up publicity from a local paper."

"Confirmed by the paper?"

"Aye. Mind you, his appointment was at ten in the morning."

"What about the boss, Harry Gilchrist?"

"Down in Glasgow."

"Where?"

"Got him on his mobile. He stayed with a friend. Strathclyde Police are confirming his alibi. He's on his road back."

"What about Freda?"

"At her desk all this morning."

Hamish rang off and went back to searching.

He and Dick drove up to the viewpoint, parked, and got out. A wind sprang up, and the weather of Sutherland went in for one of its mercurial changes. The cloud was blown into grey rags and sent flying off to the east. The blue mountains appeared, range after range of them, stretching into Sutherland. The sun shone down on the purple heather. Rowan trees danced in the brisk wind, their leaves glittering with raindrops. It has been called "the million-dollar view." Down below lay the inner arm of the Cromarty Firth. Over in the blue distance lay the Kyle of Sutherland.

"This is hopeless," moaned Dick. "I'm hungry."

"Let me think," said Hamish. "Whoever took her was in a panic. So he wouldn't go in for anything elaborate. He'd kill her and toss the body out by the road. We'd better keep looking."

To Dick's horror, Hamish said they should start going along the road on foot. "I'm tired," he wailed. "My legs won't take it."

"You should lose weight," said Hamish heartlessly. "Oh, take a seat in the car. I'll go myself."

Hamish trudged slowly along, looking to left and right.

The road began to descend. He stopped and stared around. She could be anywhere. Why had he thought of the Struie Pass? Because there's a bit of a murderer in all of us, he thought, and it's where I would have got rid of her.

At a hairpin bend in the road, he noticed a stand of silver birch and, at the base of the trees, uprooted piles of heather.

He walked over and tugged away the heather. Hannah's white face stared up at him. He bent down and felt for a pulse. It was there, but very faint. He phoned Dick and howled for the Land Rover to be brought down the pass. He phoned for a rescue helicopter, shouting that any long delay could kill her.

He then knelt down in the heather and began to apply the kiss of life. The pulse grew slightly stronger. Dick drove up. "Oh, michty me!" he cried. "Is she dead?"

"Nearly," said Hamish. "Where's that damn helicopter."

"I hear it!" said Dick. "Coming from ower there."

The helicopter landed on the road. Paramedics rushed to Hannah and put an oxygen mask over her mouth before lifting her on board. "I'll go with her," said Hamish. "Phone headquarters and say she's been found."

Hamish was joined in Strathbane Hospital by Jimmy and Blair. Blair tried to send Hamish away, but Jimmy protested. "He found the lassie. If she recovers, he'll be the first person she'll want to talk to."

The day wore on as the news of the discovery of Hannah Fleming went out over the airwaves.

Someone, it seemed, had tried to strangle her. Eventually a doctor joined them. "It looks as if she will recover," he said. "But no one is to interview her at the moment. She's still barely conscious."

"I'm hungry," said Jimmy. "Let's go to the canteen and get something, Hamish.

"I'm off," said Blair. "Phone me as soon as she's ready to speak."

*   *   *

After they had eaten, Hamish and Jimmy went back downstairs. They sent for the doctor they had seen earlier. "She has recovered consciousness," he said. "You can have a few words, but that is all."

Now, thought Hamish, we'll get the identity of this murdering bastard at last.

The doctor followed Hamish and Jimmy into the room. Hamish took one look at Hannah and cursed. He had seen death many times before and recognised it in Hannah's clay-white face.

"What's happened here?" demanded the doctor, striding to the bed. "Her tubes have been pulled out, and what's that pillow doing lying on the floor?"

"Don't touch it!" yelled Hamish as he made to pick it up. "I think someone's got in here and smothered her."

Blair soon came roaring back followed by Superintendent Daviot. Blair raged that she should never have been left alone.

"We'll get the CCTV stuff," said Jimmy, "and find out who went into her room."

"Won't do you much good," said Hamish miserably. "I took a look at the one in the corridor and it's been spray-painted black."

Blair howled with rage and cursed and stamped and then he clutched his throat and fell unconscious on the floor.

Medics rushed to bear him away. Daviot shook his silver head. "A guard should have been put on her door. This is terrible publicity. What am I to tell the press?"

Hamish finally got back to his police station at three in the morning. He could hear snores coming from Dick's bedroom. He had developed such a rage, such a personal hate for this murderer, that he felt that if Hannah had lived and had told about her night with him, he would gladly have faced the music if it got him the identity of this killer.

He undressed and went to bed, falling into an exhausted sleep haunted by dreams of the people at the factory.

In the morning, Hamish phoned Jimmy. "There's a back stair leading from the corridor outside Hannah's room," said Jimmy. "No cameras there. We're getting statements again from everyone at that factory."

"I'll be right over," said Hamish.

"I'm in charge of the case now," said Jimmy. "Blair's had a wee stroke and is being kept in. You just get on with your usual duties."

Hamish sighed after he had rung off. If Blair's condition turned out to be serious, then Jimmy saw promotion. Any kudos he would want for himself.

Dick arrived in the kitchen. "Where were you yesterday?" demanded Hamish.

"I didnae see that there was anything I could do," said Dick plaintively. "Is she going to be all right?"

"She's dead," said Hamish and told Dick what had happened, ending with, "Blair got a stroke so Jimmy has dreams of glory and I'm being asked to keep clear."

"It's a grand day," said Dick looking out of the window. "We both need a rest."

"On the contrary," said Hamish. "They'll all be concentrating on alibis. We should go over to the hospital and ask around."

"Don't you want me to stay behind and look after Sonsie and Lugs?"

"I'll take the beasts with me," said Hamish curtly. "Get your uniform on."

At the hospital, Hamish and Dick went up to the corridor outside Hannah's room and walked along until they found the back stairs and then started to walk slowly down.

"Have forensics been over this?" asked Dick uneasily. "We could be charged with mucking up a crime scene."

"They've been and gone," said Hamish. "There's fingerprint dust all over the banisters."

At the bottom of the stairs, there was a fire door. They pushed it open and found themselves at the back of the hospital. Hamish turned and scrutinised the building. "Not a camera in sight," he muttered. "Our murderer either knew about that or was lucky in his desperation."

He scanned the ground. A little way away was a small patch of earth, still damp from the previous day's rain. There was the mark of a single tyre. "Looks like a bicycle track," said Hamish. "They should have taken a cast of it."

He walked back to the fire door. "Cigarette butts all over the place," said Hamish. "This must be one of the places where the staff nip out to have cigarettes. We'll go back in and see if there's any of them in the canteen."

In the canteen, he tried to pull Dick back from heading for the service counter but Dick said, "We need to eat and get something for the beasties."

Hamish released him and then started to go round the tables where staff were having coffee. Not one admitted to having seen anything.

Dick came back with two coffees, buns, and pies for Sonsie and Lugs. Hamish gulped down his coffee and said, "You go and feed Sonsie and Lugs and then meet me round at that door. The ones in the canteen were probably not smokers. I'm going to wait there and see if anyone comes out."

Hamish waited patiently outside. After half an hour, a hospital porter came out and lit a cigarette. "Were you out here yesterday?" asked Hamish.

"Aye, but I wasnae murdering anyone."

"Did you see anyone at all?"

"Cars down on the road. I was on my own. Oh, I mind, there was a hoody on a bike just going round that corner on the left."

"What did he look like?"

"I only got a glimpse. You ken what these hoodies are like. They aye look the same."

"What colour of hoody?"

"Grey."

"Small, fat, thin?"

"Medium built, average size. It was one o' thae wee collapsible bikes folks carry around in their cars. Hood right ower his head."

"What time was this?"

"Be about dinnertime."

Correctly understanding that by dinnertime, he meant midday, Hamish asked, "That was about the time the murder was committed. Didn't you think to tell the police?"

"Didnae think."

"Did you see any other members of the staff when you were out here smoking?"

"Naw. On my lonesome."

Hamish took down his name and address and said they would be in touch with him.

Dick arrived, brushing crumbs from his regulation shirt. Hamish told him what he had found out. "I'd better phone Jimmy," he said. "We've got to find out if anyone in Cnothan owns such a cycle."

Jimmy listened in silence, and then, as if realising he might be missing out by keeping Hamish out of the investigation, said, "Get over here. I'll let you look through the statements. You might see something I've missed."

Once in Cnothan, Hamish sent Dick back to Lochdubh with his pets. The village was now swarming with press, and he didn't want any photographer snapping a picture of his wild cat and starting up arguments about the legality of having such an animal as a pet.

He found Jimmy outside the factory. "I could do with a drink," said Jimmy. "Let's go along to the Loaming. I'll go over the statements with you."

When they entered the pub, Hamish recognised Maisie Moffat, sitting at a table with some of the staff. When they saw Hamish and Jimmy, they finished their drinks and hurried out.

Jimmy ordered a double whisky for himself and an orange juice for Hamish and then settled down at the table recently vacated by the factory staff.

He put a laptop on the table and switched it on. He tossed back his drink. "Help yourself, Hamish. I need another. It was worse than interviewing the mafia. Talk about omerta!"

Hamish began to read. He had given up smoking some time ago but he suddenly longed for a cigarette. Then he found himself yearning for the cool company of Priscilla Halburton-Smythe who had acted as his Watson on so many cases. He sighed and began to concentrate.

Hannah's brother had been sedated and could not be interviewed. Pete Eskdale had been out of the factory the previous morning. He said he had gone down to Strathbane to interview a secretary as Gilchrist was complaining that the new one was no good. The applicant, a Miss Henrietta Noble, confirmed that he had called and had said he would let her know. But it left a time lag where he could have gone to the hospital. Warrants had been issued to search the premises of all suspects to look for a hooded outfit or a collapsible bicycle. A team of detectives and police were currently operating the searches.

Harry Gilchrist had returned from Glasgow after lunch the previous day. He said he had left Glasgow early in the morning and had driven straight to Lochdubh.

Freda Crichton had taken the day off sick. No witnesses. She had not called a doctor.

Maisie Moffat had taken the morning off to visit a sick friend in Bonar Bridge. Friend confirmed the visit but a gap between ten in the morning and one in the afternoon.

"What do you think?" asked Jimmy impatiently. "Have we a visiting serial killer?"

"I think we've got a panicking amateur here," said Hamish. "And a very lucky one at that. I think Fergus knew something and was blackmailing whoever. Hannah was fantasising. I'm sure of that. The trouble is that television these days gives everyone a lesson in how to do it." He shuffled the statements restlessly. "Such a cliché."

"What is?"

"Hannah's death in the hospital. How many cop dramas and real-life crime shows have portrayed someone being murdered in hospital. I've even seen one where the CCTV camera was spray-painted. It was all over the news about her press conference. She phoned her brother and told him where she was. We've got to find out who he told. She'd still be alive if he had told us. Where was he when he got the call?"

"At his desk in the factory. And worse. He shouted, 'Hannah! Where are you?' Then he wrote down the name of the hotel on a bit o' paper and put it in his desk. Anyone could have overheard him and spread the news. It couldn't have been Gilchrist. He was down in Glasgow."

"Somebody might have phoned him."

Jimmy's phone rang. He listened and then got to his feet and walked outside. When he came back in, his face was grim.

"You're to report right now to Daviot," he said. "An anonymous caller has reported that you were overheard threatening to kill Hannah Fleming. The caller also said you had dinner with her in Lochdubh and that she spent the night in the police station."

Nessie Currie, thought Hamish bleakly.

"This is mad," said Hamish. "I'm the one who found her on the Struie Pass and saved her life. Dick was with me."

"Get along with you," said Jimmy heavily. "Thank your lucky stars that Blair is still in hospital."

As Hamish waited outside the superintendent's office, he reflected that the gods were punishing him for his night with Hannah Fleming. He had accused her of vanity, but what about his own behaviour? He had been carried away by her appearance alone.

Helen, Daviot's secretary, came out of her boss's room and gave Hamish the thin malicious smile she always gave him when he was in trouble. "You're to go in now."

"This is a bad business, Macbeth," said Daviot. "We have had an anonymous report that you were heard threatening to kill Hannah Fleming and that you had dined with her and that she had spent a night at the police station. At that time, Miss Fleming was the sister of one of our suspects. Before I take this to internal affairs, I would like your version of what happened."

*   *   *

While Hamish had been on his road to Lochdubh, Dick had phoned Jimmy, looking for Hamish whose phone was switched off, and had heard what had happened. When he had rung off, he looked dismally at the cool blonde sitting at the kitchen table.

"Hamish is in bad trouble, Miss Halburton-Smythe," he said.

"Why?"

Dick rapidly told her about Hannah and the night in the police station. "It was as innocent as anything," he said. "The lassie was just too drunk to go home."

"What evening was this?"

Dick told her.

"I was up here on a flying visit," said Priscilla. "I called in to see Hamish. Hannah Fleming had already passed out. Got it?"

"Got it."

"Got to rush."

Daviot listened carefully to Hamish's long explanation. Daviot just finished when his phone rang. Hamish stood in front of the superintendent's desk, his face a picture of misery. It was obviously Daviot's wife on the phone. Daviot kept protesting he hadn't time to do any shopping and he didn't care who was coming to dinner, he was in the middle of a murder enquiry. His wife's voice at the other end squawked loudly.

At last Daviot rang off and mopped his brow. "Where was I? Yes, you are to go downstairs and write a statement and bring it back to me. You are, of course, suspended from duty and... what is it, Helen?"

"Miss Halburton-Smythe is here. She says she has urgent information concerning Macbeth."

"Show her in."

Hamish looked in surprise at Priscilla. From the blonde bell of her hair to her neat half boots, she was as beautiful and impeccable as ever.

"I called in at the police station and heard what the fuss was about and came right away. You will want my statement."

"Please take a seat, Miss Halburton-Smythe. Why should I want your statement?"

"Only that on the night Miss Fleming was at the police station, I called there late. Hamish was getting ready to bed down in the cell. Miss Fleming was already snoring her drunken head off on his bed. Hamish told me he had made a mistake taking her for dinner but that he had hoped to get a lead on some of the people at the factory."

"Is this true, Macbeth?"

"Aye, I'm afraid I've been that upset, I forgot," said Hamish.

Daviot was a snob and the word of someone like

Priscilla Halburton-Smythe was, in his opinion, to be ranked somewhere slightly below the word of God.

Priscilla said, "You were so tired, Hamish, and so upset that you had wasted time on her, that I'm not surprised you forgot my visit. I was only there a few minutes."

Daviot smiled. "This does put a different complexion on that matter. But your methods are very unorthodox, Macbeth."

"But it is those very methods that have solved so many cases in the past," put in Priscilla.

"Perhaps." The phone rang again. "I am talking to Miss Halburton-Smythe, dear," said Daviot importantly. The voice of his wife at the other end could be heard quacking loudly. When he rang off, Daviot said, "My lady wife wonders if you would care to join us for dinner this evening, Miss Halburton-Smythe?"

Priscilla smiled sweetly. "Alas, this is only another flying visit to see my parents, and they have invited Lord and Lady Pastern to dinner this evening."

Daviot looked suitably impressed.

When Priscilla and Hamish emerged from police headquarters, Hamish thanked her as she explained how Dick had told her the trouble he was in. "Are Lord and Lady Pastern really coming to dinner?" he asked.

"No, but it was the snobbiest couple of names I could think of. Let's go for a coffee. I want to hear about the case."

The wind had risen, and her blonde hair was whipped about her face. Hamish noticed when they entered the café that her hair fell back into its impeccable bell shape. I wonder how she does that? he thought.

Outside the café windows, rubbish danced in the rising gale. There had been a refuse collectors' strike.

"Sutherland has decided we have had enough of this odd good weather," said Priscilla. "Now, Hamish, begin at the beginning."

So Hamish did, giving her a concise report.

"It's got to be someone at the factory," said Priscilla when he had finished.

"I'm inclined to agree with you," said Hamish, fighting down a treacherous wonder if Priscilla ever remembered lying in his arms. As he looked at her, he thought, not for the first time, that she was like an addiction. In just the way that he was sometimes assailed with a longing for a cigarette, so he longed for the passionate Priscilla of his dreams, a Priscilla, he knew, that did not exist. That was the reason he had broken off their engagement.

"You see," said Priscilla, "it must have been someone who was on hand to find out which hotel she was staying at."

"But which one?" mourned Hamish. "You know

Cnothan. They don't talk to outsiders at the best of times."

"Jobs are hard to come by in the north," said Priscilla. "Before the recession, there was a big influx of Poles, taking on the jobs the locals wouldn't do. By the time they were prepared to do anything, the jobs had gone. The people of Cnothan are desperate that nothing should happen to that factory. What about that friend of Morag's, Celia Hedron, the flatmate in London?"

"Not a suspect. She never left London and is still there."

"But if Morag was a friend of hers and if it was a close relationship, Morag might have phoned her."

"I think I've got her number. I'll phone from outside. She's been interviewed but she might remember some small thing. Do you want to wait and hear what she says?"

"No, I've got to rush. I'm due back in London tomorrow."

"Dinner tonight?"

"Why not? I'll meet you at the Italian restaurant at eight o'clock."

Outside the café, the blustery wind sent Priscilla's hair flying about her face and whipped at her thin jacket.

Hamish's cap was torn from his head and went dancing off down the street. By the time he had recovered it, Priscilla had gone.

He climbed into the Land Rover and searched

through his records until he found a home number and mobile number for Celia Hedron. Celia was at home and sounded puzzled when he introduced himself. "I don't know that I can add anything to what I have already told the police," she said.

"You have been told she was pregnant?"

"Yes. It was a great shock. The Morag I knew had no interest in men."

"Would she be tempted by money? Say she came across some rich man."

"I don't think so. I know she did want a baby. But she had planned to get one by artificial insemination."

"Any record of that?"

"No, Scotland Yard checked everywhere."

"Did she talk about people in the factory?"

"Very dismissively," said Celia. "She said they were a bunch of morons. But she would enjoy that."

"Why?"

"I loved Morag but I wasn't blind to her faults. It was almost as if she was compelled to look down on people to bolster up her self-worth. She was a good graphic artist, but there are lots of them around and she couldn't get work. The idea of going up to the Highlands amused her."

"Didn't she mention any men at all?"

"Look, we had a quarrel about a month before she was murdered. I had been getting a bit tired of her high-and-mighty attitude. I have a prospect of a good job with an advertising company. She went very sour when I told her and said, 'I don't think your work will be up to it. Aren't you afraid?' I told her to find somewhere else to live. But she got the job before she found anything else. I told her not to speak to me again. But she did. She had to brag about the hypnotist and how someone had drugged her. Did you say your name was Hamish Macbeth?"

"Yes."

"Morag said you really fancied her."

"Not even the slightest bit," said Hamish coldly. "Write down my number and if you can think of any little thing, let me know."

At the police station, Dick chortled gleefully when Hamish told him of Priscilla's rescue.

"A grand lassie," said Dick. "Oh, while you were out, I got a call. A woman over in Southey says her man went out last night and didnae come home. I told her to wait a bit."

"What's his name?"

"Bob Macdonald. A crofter."

"We'd better get over there and look into it. He could be lying out in his fields."

"Och, do we have to? He'll probably be home when we get there."

"Let's hope so," said Hamish curtly. "Get your uniform on. And switch that television off!"

*   *   *

Southey was more of a hamlet than a village, a huddle of houses in front of a curve of white sand. Great Atlantic waves were crashing on the beach, their tops whipped back by the gale.

The Macdonalds' croft house was on a rise above the village. As they drove up, a small round woman with greying hair came out to meet them.

She led the way into a small parlour. The room smelled of furniture polish. It was obviously only used for special occasions.

"When did you last see him?" asked Hamish.

"It would be just afore teatime. About five o'clock. He was just going out to check the fences, but he never came back."

"Have the locals been out looking for him?"

Tears welled up in her eyes. "They won't move. They don't like him. Our neighbour, Bella Robertson, left him her house and croft in her will. Her son and daughter are furious and they're trying to break the will. Everyone's sided with them."

"Would anyone attack him?"

"We're all God-fearing people here," she said. "No one would dream of it."

"What about the sheepdog?"

"Came back on his own. I took the dog back out and searched the fields."

"We'll go and have a look."

*   *   *

Hamish and Dick searched fields high and wide with the sheepdog, Cally, following at their heels.

"He could be anywhere," groaned Dick, puffing and panting.

"We need a bloodhound," said Hamish. "You would think Cally would find his master. Let's try the beach."

"Can I no' just sit in the Land Rover?" pleaded Dick. "Your ain beasties will be wanting a bit of air."

"Oh, go on," said Hamish impatiently.

He strode over the fields and down onto the beach, his boots sinking in the soft sand. Out to the west, black clouds were beginning to pile up. Ribbons of white sand blown by the wind snaked in front of him. He walked to where the cliffs began at the west end of the beach. He climbed up to the top of the cliffs and stood, holding on to his hat, scanning round about through a pair of binoculars.

And then, on the top of a flat rock, buffeted by the rising tide, he saw what looked at first like a pile of rags. Then with a lurch in his stomach, he found he was looking at a body.

He started to climb down towards the rock. The large rock was sloping on the shore side, rising to its flat top where a man lay. Hamish scrambled up. The man had been tied down with ropes held by spikes driven into the rock. Hamish felt for a pulse and found a faint flicker. The tide was coming in fast and the man's clothes were soaked. Hamish took out a knife and cut the ropes. He phoned Dick and shouted that he needed air-sea rescue and a defibrillator out of the Land Rover and warm blankets. He told him where he was.

The tide was coming in. A great wave crashed against the rock. He gently sledged the man down the slope of the rock and then, his muscles cracking with the strain, lifted him up and laid him on a flat piece of shingle at the base of the cliffs, out of the wind and away from the rising tide.

Dick arrived and came scrambling to join him, followed by Mrs. Macdonald. "It's my man," she wailed. "Is he dead?"

"I'm trying to keep him alive." Hamish opened the man's clothes and applied the pads of the defibrillator.

"He's still with us," muttered Hamish. "I hear that helicopter. Get on the beach and signal to them, Dick."

Hamish sighed with relief as paramedics rushed up with a stretcher. He was carried to the helicopter that had landed on the beach. His wife followed him into the helicopter.

"Now," said Hamish, taking out his phone. "Let's see who was trying to kill him."

After he had finished calling headquarters and asked them to find out the addresses of Bella Robertson's son and daughter, he retreated to the Land Rover and waited.

"This is a bad business," said Dick. "What's happened to Sutherland? I've got some emergency rations in the back and a flask of coffee. I don't know about you, but I could do with something."

After half an hour, Jimmy phoned to say that he was on the road. Bella Robertson's son and daughter shared a flat in Braikie. But Hamish was ordered to wait where he was.

At last Jimmy arrived with three detectives and a squad of policemen followed closely by the forensic van. Hamish took them to the rock and pointed out the ropes and spikes. They retreated before a great wave as the tide nearly engulfed the rock.

"The idea," said Hamish, "must have been to leave him until he drowned, then come back and remove the evidence of the spikes and rope and maybe tip him down the rock so that it would look like natural causes. It's a miracle the man survived at all."

Police and detectives then spread out to interview the villagers. Jimmy suggested that he, Hamish, and Dick should go to Braikie to interview the son and daughter. "Neither of them's married," he said. "Dorothy Robertson works in a local café and Ian Robertson is at home on disability."

He peered into the back of the Land Rover. "Do you have to take thae beasts with you everywhere, Hamish?"

"They're not bothering anyone," said Hamish crossly. "Let's get on the road."

The son and daughter lived in a small bungalow on the edge of the town.

Hamish glanced at his watch as Jimmy rang the doorbell. Six o'clock! Would he ever be able to meet Priscilla for dinner?

The door was opened by a scrawny woman in her thirties. Her mouth was turned down at the corners, witness to the highland curse of getting all one's teeth removed after the first toothache. She had protruding brown eyes under heavy brows and hair scraped back from her face.

"Police!" said Jimmy. "May we come in?"

"I was just going out. I'm due to start my shift."

"You're not going anywhere," snapped Jimmy. "If you don't let us in, we'll take you to police headquarters."

She stood back and let them past. She opened the door to a cluttered living room. A man, presumably her brother, Ian, was sitting in a wheelchair in front of the television.

"What's this about?" she demanded. Her brother switched off the television and moved his chair round. He had thinning hair combed in strips over a pink scalp and a long, lugubrious face.

"Bob Macdonald was found tied to a rock on the beach in Southey."

"That's awful," said Dorothy. "But what's it got to do with us?"

"You are reported as being bitter that Bella Robertson left the croft to Bob Macdonald. You are contesting the will."

"It wasn't fair. But what the hell's it got to do with us?"

"Where were you around five o'clock yesterday afternoon?" asked Jimmy.

"Here! With my brother. He's disabled as you can see. How could either of us go up to Southey and overpower Bob and tie him to a rock?"

Jimmy's phone rang. He went outside to answer it.

"Why are you disabled?" asked Hamish.

"I was working on construction and took a fall," said Ian.

"And when was this?"

"This time last year, over at the new office building on the other side of the town."

Jimmy came back. "Bob Macdonald was struck a blow on the head, rendering him unconscious."

"We were here all the time!" shrieked Dorothy. "Now get out!"

"We'll be back with a search warrant," said Jimmy.

Chapter Seven

Secret guilt by silence is betrayed.

—John Dryden

Outside, Jimmy said, "I'm going for a drink. They'll phone me when the search warrant is being brought over. But it cannae be them. Someone strong had to have moved that body."

"Ian Robertson's got powerful arms on him," said Hamish.

"Aye, but he's in a wheelchair."

"Jimmy, I think we ought to wait a bit in case they make a run for it."

"I need a drink."

"I've a flask of brandy in the back of the vehicle."

"Oh, well fish it out."

"We'd better look as if we're going away," said Hamish. "We can park round the corner and watch from the end of the street. Their house is a bit isolated so there'll be no nosy neighbours to tell them we're still here."

Half an hour dragged past. Then the door opened and Dorothy appeared carrying two suitcases, which she put into the back of a Subaru estate car.

"Wait!" urged Hamish as Jimmy would have run forward. "Wait for the brother."

The door opened and Ian appeared pushing his wheelchair, which he loaded in the back.

"That's it!" cried Jimmy. "Let's get them!"

Ian fought hard until Hamish was able to disable him, bring him down, and clip on a pair of handcuffs. Jimmy charged him with faking a disability and his sister with enabling him. He called for backup.

When brother and sister were taken away, the search warrant arrived, along with the Scenes of Crime Operatives. Hamish and Jimmy waited outside. Back at the end of the street, Dick took out a folding canvas chair and sat down, placidly watching the dog and cat run around.

"Do I have to wait?" asked Hamish, glancing at his watch.

"You'd better," said Jimmy. "If they don't find any evidence, we're stuffed."

Hamish felt he should phone Priscilla but kept putting it off, hoping he would still have time to get to the restaurant by eight o'clock.

"It's a wonder none of the villagers in Southey saw anything," said Jimmy.

"You would have to stand on the cliff and look down to see that rock," said Hamish. "They probably knocked Bob on the head and put him in the wheelchair. You know what teatime in the Highlands is like. Nobody moves outdoors."

Jimmy's phone rang again. When he had finished his call, he said, "Good news. Bob Macdonald is going to recover. Thank God it was a warm night or he'd have surely died of cold and exposure. So that should wrap things up."

"I'd better get back to the police station and type up my report," said Hamish.

"All right. Off you go. Oh, wait a bit. They've found something."

Hamish fretted while Jimmy talked to a white-coated figure, carrying a box. "Spikes!" he said, returning to Hamish.

"Great," said Hamish. "Come along, Dick."

Hamish raced to Lochdubh. His report would have to wait. He left Dick and his pets at the station and hurried along to the restaurant, still wearing his uniform.

Priscilla smiled as he joined her at the table. "It must have been something urgent," she said. "But you're only about ten minutes late."

After they had placed their order and got rid of Willie, who showed a desire to hang over the table, Hamish described the two cases.

"How did you guess the man in the wheelchair was faking?" she asked.

"They were the likeliest suspects and sooner or later we would have traced them back to the attempted murder. But I got this feeling about him. Something bad. I wish I could get the same feeling about some of the suspects in the Cnothan murders."

"Maybe," suggested Priscilla, "you've been looking at them all at once. Say you were to go back and talk to each of your suspects individually and see if you can sense something about them."

"I'll try that," said Hamish. "I can't sit back and just let a murderer roam loose. How are things with you?"

"Pretty much the same."

"Is the recession hitting the hotel?"

"Not at the moment. The whole hotel has been booked up by the executives of the Northern Scottish Bank and their wives."

"But that's wicked!" exclaimed Hamish. "The Tommel Castle Hotel is expensive, and that bank's already had to be bailed out by the taxpayer."

"That's banks for you," said Priscilla. "They live in a different world. They go on like the French royal family before the revolution. The press have got wind of it, so there'll be another scandal. It's cynical of me, but it will do the hotel no harm. They'll photograph everything and exaggerate the luxury. How is Elspeth?"

"I haven't heard a word."

They talked amiably through the rest of the meal about people they knew and old murder cases.

After dinner, he escorted her to her car. Overcome by a sudden impulse, he took her in his arms and kissed her passionately. For one glorious moment, he felt her response, and then she went rigid in his arms. He released her.

"Enough of that nonsense, Hamish," she said. Priscilla got in her car and drove off, leaving him standing miserably on the waterfront.

He made his way slowly back to the police station.

"What's up with you?" asked Dick.

"You give your heart to someone," said Hamish bitterly, "and all they can say is 'Enough of that nonsense, Hamish.'"

Hamish spent the following morning avoiding the press who wanted details of what they were calling the Wheelchair Murder. Fortunately, Superintendent Daviot—always keen to appear on television—arrived in Lochdubh to hold a press conference on the waterfront.

Hamish and Dick drove off to Cnothan with Sonsie and Lugs in the back.

When they arrived at the factory, a busload of tourists was just arriving. Hamish watched them walking in. He suddenly wished he knew more about Morag's past. It would be easy for someone to arrive as a tourist, separate from the group, and waylay her. But the procurator fiscal's report claimed she had been killed elsewhere. Morag had no immediate family. A second cousin had seen to the funeral arrangements.

He decided to start with Pete Eskdale. It was nearly lunchtime but he doubted Pete would want to eat in the factory canteen.

While Dick took the animals off for some exercise, Hamish waited by Pete's car. Promptly at one o'clock he came out. He stiffened slightly at the sight of Hamish and then arranged his features in a friendly smile.

"Can I help you?"

"Just a wee talk," said Hamish.

"Join me for lunch? I was just about to drive over to the Tommel Castle Hotel."

"I doubt if you'll find a place," said Hamish. "It's full of press and bankers."

"Damn! The food in Cnothan is vile. Oh, well, I suppose it'll have to be the workers' canteen. Join me?"

"I'll have a coffee."

When they were settled at a table, Hamish studied the personnel officer. His suit, shirt, and silk tie looked expensive. Had he been fiddling the books? He had claimed that his lottery win had been dissipated by alimony. But Geordie Fleming did the accounts.

"It's like this," began Hamish. "I can't leave these murders unsolved. Morag's murder must have been something to do with her pregnancy. Or maybe she found out something else."

"No use asking me," said Pete. "I've batted my brains. Look. I know all these people at the factory. I know their backgrounds. Not one of them is capable of one murder, let alone three."

"It would surprise you how often innocent-looking people can turn out to be villains."

Pete nervously smoothed back his ginger hair. He poked a fork into a square of lasagne. "This canteen is good for the figure," he said. "Can barely eat the stuff."

"When you were in London, interviewing Morag, did you sleep with her?"

"No, I did not. And that's been checked out with about all the staff at the hotel I stayed at. I mean, she thought she was God's gift, but she was no looker. I'm not so desperate that I have to get my leg over women who look like Morag Merrilea."

"What about Hannah Fleming?"

"Never touched her. Thought about it. Took her to lunch. What a bore she turned out to be!"

And I never knew until it was too late, thought Hamish with a sharp pang of guilt.

He remembered Priscilla's advice. Pete was shifty about something. But people often got nervous and irrationally guilty when questioned by the police.

"How is the factory doing?" he asked.

"We're doing great. We're going to bring out an up-market line. Freda Crichton's a genius. We plan to hold a fashion show down in Inverness in the autumn. I've employed a publicist. Wee lassie called Joan Friend. Bags of oomph."

"Where did you get her from?"

"I spotted her in Inverness. She was hosting a fund-raiser for Scottish soldiers injured in Afghanistan. Real livewire."

"I would like to meet her," said Hamish, thinking that a pair of fresh eyes at the factory might have noticed something.

"She doesn't start until next week."

"Have you got her address?"

"She's right here in Cnothan, settling in. You'll find her at Cairn cottage in the High Street, right opposite the butchers. What do you want to talk to her about?"

"I'd like her opinion of people in the factory."

"She hasn't had time to get to know anyone."

"You never know."

"I wish you'd leave us alone," said Pete, pushing his plate of food away from him. "We're a great bunch of people."

"I'm convinced that somewhere in that great bunch of people there is a murderer," said Hamish. He got up and left, leaving Pete staring after him.

Once outside, Hamish could not see the Land Rover. He started to walk towards the High Street. It was a steel-grey day. A light breeze ruffled the pewter-coloured waters of the loch. Long black streamers of cloud were moving across the sky from the west. Hamish could smell rain.

In the High Street, he could see the Land Rover parked outside the café. Dick was no doubt eating as usual and finding food for Sonsie and Lugs. He decided to leave him to it, although feeling guilty that he had fallen into the bad habit of treating Dick more like a convenient animal minder rather than a policeman.

Cairn cottage was actually a thirties-style pebble-dashed two-storey building. It fronted directly onto the street. He rang the bell and waited.

The door was opened by a small figure with curly black hair and rosy cheeks.

"Miss Friend?"

"That's me. What's up?"

"Nothing serious," said Hamish soothingly. "I heard you were about to start work at the factory. I am investigating the recent murders."

"You'd better come in. It's a mess. I'm still unpacking. Come through to the kitchen."

The kitchen looked frozen in the early fifties. There was a Belfast sink with brass taps. An old Hoover washing machine, the kind you emptied by putting a hose in the sink, crouched in one corner. The gas cooker had a door of chipped green enamel. Wooden shelves painted sulphureous yellow held a variety of dishes, not one of them matching. In the middle of the linoleum-covered floor was a white plastic-topped table surrounded by four white plastic chairs.

"I've taken the place furnished," said Joan. "It's all pretty awful. Want coffee? I brought my own machine."

Hamish studied her while she prepared the coffee. She was wearing a faded blue T-shirt and worn jeans. Her figure was plump. She had very wide blue eyes and a generous mouth.

When the coffee was ready, they sat down, facing each other. "So what's it all about?" she asked.

"It's about these murders," said Hamish. "You're new. I was hoping you might be able to find out something about the people at the factory."

"Be a police nark?"

"That sounds bad. I'm at my wit's end. I just want you to keep your eyes open and see if you can *sense* anything about anyone."

"I suppose I can do that," she said slowly. "I took the job because the fashions are exciting. It's an awful thing to say but the murders won't do us any harm. It'll bring more press than would normally be interested in a provincial fashion show. Is there anyone you want me to take a good look at?"

"No one in particular. I need someone to take a new look at all the people there. Here's my card.

Phone me about the least little thing you think might be helpful."

When Hamish walked back down the High Street, he considered joining Dick who was still in the café, but was suddenly overtaken by a burning resentment towards the man.

How could he, Hamish Macbeth, ever settle down and get married with Dick around, playing housewife? He felt crowded and wanted his old solitary life back, where he could dream of some woman coming into his life.

Instead, he went back to the factory and asked to speak to Freda Crichton. He was led through to a studio at the back of the factory.

Freda was working on designs. She hailed him by saying, "I've got my own studio now. It's great. What brings you?"

"Still working on the murders," said Hamish. He sat down next to her. He decided he could not imagine such as Freda committing three murders.

"I wish you'd find the bastard that killed Morag," said Freda. "She turned out to be a two-faced liar, but I still miss her. Now that it's out that I'm a lesbian, they look at me as if I had two heads. Fortunately, they need my designs."

"If it should turn out to be someone in this place, who would you select?" asked Hamish.

She scowled ferociously and then said, "Pete Eskdale."

"Why him?"

"I've been thinking a lot about it. Why should he hire someone all the way from London? I think he's the father of her child."

"But the London end was thoroughly checked out. He took her for dinner. He went back to his hotel and she went back to her digs. Nothing there."

Hamish's mobile phone rang. He moved over to a corner of the studio to answer it.

When he returned to Freda, he said, "Good news! We've overturned the decision not to take blood samples. We can go ahead. Now we'll find out who the father is!"

Happily, Hamish returned to the café and collected Dick. There was no point in interviewing all the suspects again until the tests were over and the results came through.

Normally, it would take quite a time for DNA results, but a rush job was ordered. A month later as purple heather covered the moors and the flanks of the great Sutherland mountains, Hamish received the news. Not one man tested had turned out to be the father of Morag's baby. He found it hard to believe.

Hamish decided to investigate the London end for himself. He would need to take a week's holiday and go unofficially. He felt if he could have a face-to-face talk with Celia Hedron, he might just find out something new.

He had to admit that it was grand to have Dick on hand to look after his beloved pets. Usually when he went away, Sonsie and Lugs would go out looking for him. But they were fond of Dick and he was sure they would stay with him.

He phoned Celia and arranged an appointment. Before he left the Highlands, he had an impulse to go and visit the seer, Angus Macdonald. He did not believe much in Angus's psychic abilities, but knew he did have a miraculous way of finding out useful gossip.

Angus always expected some sort of gift. Dick had won a fast-boiling electric kettle in a pub quiz in Strathbane. They already had one. With Dick's permission, Hamish packed it up and headed for the seer's cottage.

Angus, looking more like one of the minor prophets than ever with his grey beard and long shaggy locks, was delighted with the present. "Come ben," he said. "You'll have come about the murders."

Hamish sat down in a high-backed chair by the smouldering peat fire and took off his cap. "Heard anything useful?" he said.

Angus sat down in his battered armchair on the other side of the fire and closed his eyes. "I will consult the spirits," he said.

"Och, Angus, drop the malarkey and just..."

"Shh! It's all about the money," he crooned. "Herself liked money. Wanted a baby but didnae like the men."

"Angus, how...?"

"Quiet! Ach, couldnae ye keep your mouth shut? They've gone."

The seer opened his eyes and studied Hamish. "Well, you'll be wanting to get married, but good luck. You'll need it. Quite a good few folk will want to stop ye."

"And who am I going to marry?" asked Hamish cynically.

"Thon lassie, Elspeth Grant."

"Havers. I havenae seen her in ages."

"Oh, but you will."

"Angus, you hear gossip. What's going on at that factory?"

"If you hadnae have chased the spirits off, I could ha' told ye."

Hamish got to his feet. "I've a good mind to take that kettle back."

"Why? You've got another one," said Angus.

"How did you know...? Oh, never mind."

The following day, Hamish packed an overnight bag, and got Dick to drive him to Inverness airport.

When he arrived in London, he found the weather

was warm and he had to remove the sweater he was wearing under his jacket and stow it in his bag.

Celia Hedron lived in the top half of a house in Gospel Oak. She turned out to be a slightly built, wispy girl, with fine fair flyaway hair and pale eyes.

"It's a shame you've come all this way," she said. "I've been racking my brain, but I can't think of anything."

"All the men at the factory have been tested," said Hamish. "Not one of them turns out to be the father of Morag's baby. Would there possibly have been someone before she left London?"

"We were maintaining a cold silence. I kept out of her way as much as possible. Just before she left, she went out to some party at Giles Armitage's studio. She couldn't help crowing about it because I hadn't been invited. Giles was a student at the same time as us. Rich daddy, which is why he can afford a studio."

"Why didn't you mention this before?"

"Didn't seem important."

"Have you got Armitage's address?"

"Yes, I'll get it for you."

Hamish tucked the slip of paper with the address in his pocket and questioned her further, but she could not add anything to what she had already told him.

Giles Armitage's flat was in Fulham at the top of a tall white stuccoed house. He turned out to look more like a City broker than an artist. He was tall and slim with thinning brown hair, a pleasant face, and small black eyes. He was dressed in a Jermyn Street striped shirt and tailored trousers.

When Hamish introduced himself and said he was asking questions about Morag Merrilea, to his surprise, Giles said, "What's she been up to?"

"Where have you been, laddie?" exclaimed Hamish. He told him about Morag's murder.

"I've been visiting friends in Brazil," said Giles. "I never bothered to read the papers when I was away. I only got back yesterday. Poor cow! She came to one of my parties the evening before she was due to take up a job in the Highlands. Wait a bit! I've just been going through my mail and I think there's one from her. I haven't opened it yet."

"Open it now!" commanded Hamish.

He went over to a desk at the window and flicked through a pile of mail. "This looks like it. Postmarked Cnothan. Let's see. 'Dear Giles. Surprise. You're going to be a fa...'"

He turned quite white and the letter fell from his nervous fingers to the floor. Hamish snatched it up.

He read: "Dear Giles. Surprise. You're going to be a father. I'll bring the baby up on my own but I shall expect you to pay maintenance. That was quite a night we had. I tried to phone you but got no reply and some friends of yours said you were out of the country. Contact me when you get back. Love and kisses, Morag."

"It was just a one-night stand," said Giles. "I can't believe it. I was drunk. She waited behind after everyone else had gone. She was all over me."

"Didn't you use any protection?" asked Hamish.

"She said she was on the pill."

"I'll need to tell the Yard," said Hamish. "You'll need to give a DNA sample. I hope you've got a good alibi."

"Let me see," said Giles desperately. "My God! Let me think. I got up the following morning with a blinding hangover and she'd gone. I felt awful. I mean, I didn't fancy her one bit. Two days later, I left for Brazil. I've still got the tickets and my friends—I'll give you their address—will vouch for the fact that I was out there the whole time."

Hamish went outside and phoned Celia Hedron and gave her the news and then begged her to tell Scotland Yard that she had asked him to call on her if he was ever in London; otherwise they would be furious if they thought he had been poaching on their territory. Then he phoned Jimmy with the news and told him to contact Scotland Yard. To avoid upsetting the Metropolitan Police, Hamish retreated to Lochdubh to wait for results.

Two weeks later he received the news that Giles

Armitage was indeed the father of Morag's unborn child but that his alibi was solid. There was absolutely no way he could have been in the Highlands of Scotland or anywhere in the British Isles to commit the murders.

"And so that's that," said Jimmy, moving his chair aside in Hamish's kitchen to let Dick hang new curtains up at the windows. "Gingham," said Jimmy with a grin. "Very folksy. When are you pair getting married?"

"She could have slept with someone else and then told whoever that the baby was his," said Hamish.

"Dangerous thing to do these days," said Jimmy, "when anyone can buy a paternity kit from the chemists."

"Not necessarily. What good's a paternity kit without the child?" asked Hamish. "Can be done without the mother but not without the child. I'd like to go over Peter Eskdale's alibi again."

"Waste of space. All the alibis have been gone over and over."

"According to our chief."

"How's Blair?"

"Out of hospital and seemingly indestructible. Off the booze, which means he's in an even fouler temper than usual. Something's got to break. Someone somewhere knows something."

"Whoever the murderer is," said Hamish, "it's some

lucky, panicking amateur. What if thon hotel where Hannah was picked up had CCTV cameras that worked? What if someone had been driving along the Struie Pass when the body was being dumped?"

"I'd best be off," said Jimmy. "Other cases. Drugs, drugs, and more drugs. It's been a grand summer but the air's getting a bit nippy."

After he had gone, Hamish whistled to his pets and took them for a walk along the waterfront. The wind was screaming down the loch, sending little whitecaps scurrying along the tops of the waves. The mountains reared up like steel engravings, every gully and crevice clearly marked, a sign of rain to come.

He had a sudden impulse to talk to his friend Angela Brodie, but before he reached the doctor's cottage, he was waylaid by the minister's wife, Mrs. Wellington, large and tweedy as ever.

"We haven't seen you in church," she boomed. "You have not solved these dreadful murders over in Cnothan. You should think of asking Him for help."

"Yes, yes," said Hamish impatiently.

"And you should go and see Mairie Torrich. She's been taken to Braikie hospital."

"What's up with her? I barely know the woman. Why should I go and see her?"

"Because she tried to commit suicide. Didn't you hear? Well, she did hush it up. She tried to hang herself but didn't make a good job of it and got a bad case of whiplash."

"Why did she try to hang herself?"

"That's what I want to find out. She won't tell anyone. Suicide's a crime. Find out. She's a staunch member of the church."

After Mrs. Wellington had bustled off, Hamish sighed. He would have to leave a visit to Angela to another day. Someone on his beat had tried to kill herself. It was his duty to look into the matter and make sure no one had driven her to it.

He drove to Braikie hospital and was ushered into a small ward where the frail figure of Mairie lay. She was a thin, pale woman in her fifties with greying hair and neat features.

She flinched when she saw Hamish and said hoarsely, "Have you come to arrest me?"

"No, Mairie. I would like to know what drove you to do such a thing."

A tear ran down her cheek. "I don't want to talk about it," she whispered.

"Something or someone must have driven you to it," said Hamish gently. "Look, I'm not taking notes." He stood up and drew the curtains round the bed. "Just you tell Hamish. You'll feel better if you get it off your chest."

She began to cry. Hamish found a box of tissues and handed it to her and then waited patiently.

At last, she sobbed and said, "It was the shame. I'd always been respectable. I've always gone to church. It was the baking competition."

"Go on," urged Hamish, wondering if she had tried to poison someone.

"I baked a sponge cake and for the first time in my life, it was a mess. I-I w-went over to Tarry's Cakes in Invergordon and I b-bought one. And I won first prize. I hadn't expected to win. I couldn't tell anyone. Then Mrs. Macleod's niece came visiting from Invergordon. Mrs. Macleod brought her along to the Mothers' Union. She looked at me and said, 'I've seen you before—in Tarry's Cakes. You were buying one o' their famous sponge cakes. No one makes a sponge cake like Tarry.' Well, the others gave me odd looks. Nessie Currie said, 'Miss Torrich can bake just as well. She won first prize with her sponge cake.'

"Oh, they all looked at me *so*. I wanted to sink through the floor. I've always been a respectable body. I couldn't bear it. Lochdubh seemed full of accusing eyes, everywhere I went. I decided to end it all but I couldn't even get that right." She began to cry again.

"Be back in a minute," said Hamish. He went out into the corridor and phoned Dick. "Have you heard any gossip about Mairie Torrich putting a shop cake into the baking competition?"

"Not a word."

"So don't talk about this to anyone. Right?"

"Okay. But what ... ?"

"I'll tell you later."

He went back to Mairie and waited until she had finished crying. "It's nothing but your guilty conscience," he said. "No one suspects a thing. Just get better and forget about it. But why try to kill yourself over something so trivial?"

"I've always been a respectable body, someone people could trust. There's nothing worse in the world than to lose respectability."

"Havers!" said Hamish. "There's war, famine, and pestilence for a start."

"You don't understand!" she wailed.

"I'm beginning to. What did you tell the hospital psychiatrist?"

"I haven't seen him. I said I bumped my car and that's how I got whiplash."

"Why wasn't I called?"

"Mrs. Wellington found me. She said it would be better to stick to the whiplash story."

"Mrs. Wellington sent me along. She thought someone had driven you to it. We'd better just say you were depressed."

"Maybe I should confess."

"I think you've taken the whole thing too seriously. There's cheating goes on all over the Highlands. It's part of our genetic make-up, like telling lies and poaching," said Hamish cheerfully.

She smiled at him mistily. "How can I ever thank you? You are so strong, so kind." She reached out to take his hand. Hamish smiled nervously and backed off.

"No thanks needed." He fled out of the ward.

Back in Lochdubh, he made his way to the manse. Mrs. Wellington stared at him when he explained that Mairie had been severely depressed.

"I don't know what's up with folk these days," complained Mrs. Wellington. "We never used to hear about depression. People just pulled themselves together and got on with things."

"It's caused by a fault in the brain," said Hamish. "She'll need a lot of kindness."

"Oh, all right. But I've never heard the like!"

Hamish then called on Angela Brodie. The doctor's wife was working on her latest novel.

"Am I interrupting you?" asked Hamish.

"Glad to take a break," said Angela. "Move a cat and sit down."

Hamish lifted one of Angela's cats off a kitchen chair and sat down opposite her. "Something's puzzling me," he said. "I'll need to tell you in strict confidence."

"Go ahead. Want some coffee?"

"No thanks," said Hamish, knowing from experience that Angela's coffee was as bad as her baking. He told her about Mairie's attempt at suicide, and ended by saying, "Doesn't that seem daft to you?"

Angela pushed a flyaway wisp of hair out of her eyes. "Not really. Look, Mairie is not married. The church and all its activities are her whole life. If she were Chinese, you would say she was suffering from loss of face. You spend too much time with criminals, Hamish. To some village people, loss of respectability is the worst thing that could happen to them. And it's not just maiden ladies in villages. There have been cases where some businessman goes bankrupt and kills his family and then himself because he can't face the shame."

"You've given me something to think about," said Hamish slowly.

He went back to the police station office and got out his notes on the suspects.

Geordie Fleming. Had he been cooking the books? Had Strathbane done an audit of the accounts? But surely he would hardly kill his own sister. On the other hand, this murderer had been driven insane—by the threat, surely, of some sort of exposure. Morag liked money. Morag could have phoned any man she had had a subsequent relationship with and claimed that he was the father of her child and asked him to pay up.

Pete Eskdale. Hamish favoured Eskdale as a prime suspect. There was a raffishness about him. But he was not married. Even if he had slept with Morag, would he care? Had he had his fingers in the till?

Freda Crichton. She had been deeply in love with Morag. What if her reaction to his story of Morag's pregnancy had been an act?

Then there was the boss, Harry Gilchrist. Where was his wife? Hamish decided it was time to call on her. She might have some insight into the character of the people in the factory.

Chapter Eight

I am past thirty, and three parts iced over.

—Matthew Arnold

Hamish walked up the front drive and rang the doorbell of the Gilchrists' villa. Sean Carmichael, the odd job man, answered the door.

"Is Mrs. Gilchrist at home?" asked Hamish.

"No. Herself is still in foreign parts."

"She's been away an awfy long time."

"Herself aye likes the travel."

"And where is she now?"

"Ask the boss. He got a postcard yesterday."

Back outside the villa, Hamish phoned Harry Gilchrist. "I wonder if I could drop in and see you," he said.

"What about? I seem to have been answering police questions for years. Besides, I'm busy."

"I actually wanted to ask you about your wife."

"What's she got to do with anything?"

"Mrs. Gilchrist has been abroad for a long time."

"My wife likes to travel. I have just received a post-card from her. Up to before she went, she had been working hard, helping me in the business. I felt she deserved a break."

"Where is she now?"

"This is police harassment. I shall speak to your superiors." He rang off.

Now, that is very interesting, thought Hamish. I'm going to see him anyway.

He was just parking outside the factory when his phone rang. It was Superintendent Daviot. "What on earth are you playing at, harassing Mr. Gilchrist," demanded Daviot.

"I just wanted to find out where his wife was," said Hamish.

"What has that got to do with anything? Mr. Gilchrist is a pillar of the community. He is a member of my lodge. His wife likes to travel. End of story. Do not trouble him and that's an order."

"Yes, sir," said Hamish meekly.

Hamish rang off and thought for a moment. Then he called Joan Friend. "Would you like to do a bit of detecting for me?"

"I've a lot to do arranging this show. Just as long as it doesn't take up too much time," said Joan.

"Harry Gilchrist got a postcard from his wife. It might be in his desk. Could you get into his office on some pretext and have a look?"

"He should be knocking off for lunch soon. I'll try then. Where are you?"

"I'm outside, but I'll go to the café in the High Street. Meet me there if you get anything."

In the café, Hamish wondered whether to buy some food for his pets and then remembered he had left them with Dick. He sometimes felt that Sonsie and Lugs were becoming fonder of Dick than they were of himself and experienced an odd pang of jealousy. Half an hour went by while he ate a dry ham sandwich and drank as much as he could of a truly horrible cup of coffee. He was just beginning to wonder whether she would come when the door of the café opened and she walked in.

"Any luck?" asked Hamish.

"Yes, I took a copy."

"Good girl. Let's see it."

She had copied both sides of a postcard. One side showed a view of Tallinn in Estonia. On the other side was a scrawled message: "Be home soon. Lovely place here. At the President Hotel. Will phone you tonight. Love and kisses, Brenda."

"What's this all about?" asked Joan.

"At the moment, I'm just thinking of this and that. Notice anything in particular about the folk at the factory?"

"I've hardly finished unpacking," she said. "Look, I just haven't got the time."

"All right," said Hamish huffily. He had become used to his female friends rushing to help him.

"Got to go!" She dashed off. Hamish stared down at the copy of the postcard. An idea began to form in his head. If he could take a weekend off and get Dick to cover for him, he might be able to book a cheap break to Tallinn. He had a sudden longing to see the mysterious Brenda Gilchrist for himself.

Tallinn, the capital of Estonia, is a small walled city, a carefully preserved mediaeval gem. A cold wind was blowing off the Baltic Sea as he made his way to the President Hotel through the narrow cobbled streets.

He was told at the reception desk that Mrs. Gilchrist was out and so he settled down in an armchair near the door to wait. He had obtained a photo of a staff party at the factory. Standing beside her husband was Brenda, a tall, rangy woman with a mass of brown hair.

Hamish began to feel sleepy and his eyelids were beginning to close when he suddenly heard the receptionist saying, "That gentleman over there is waiting for you."

She walked over to him. Hamish got to his feet. No glasses now, he thought. Contact lenses.

"Mrs. Gilchrist?"

"Yes, who are you?"

"My name is Hamish Macbeth. I am police sergeant in Lochdubh. I just happened to be here for the weekend and I remembered someone told me you were holidaying here and thought I would have a wee word."

"About the murders? I've been away the whole time. I can't help you."

"Maybe we should sit down," suggested Hamish.

"I haven't got the time and I haven't anything to tell you. Goodbye."

She turned on her heel and walked away.

Now, that's odd, thought Hamish, sitting down again. A normal reaction would be curiosity. But she's on the defence and I could swear there was a glimmer of fear in her eyes. What type of wife is it anyway who travels and travels and never goes home?

He took out a notebook and began to scribble in it questions such as: "What kind of woman is Brenda Gilchrist? What type of character? What's her background? Is she from Cnothan originally? Or does she have money of her own?"

He closed his notebook and sat for a while lost in thought. Suddenly he became aware of someone looming over him. He looked up. Brenda Gilchrist was glaring down at him.

"I have telephoned my husband. He has contacted your superior officer, Mr. Daviot. You are to report to him on your return." And before Hamish could say anything, she marched out of the hotel.

He hesitated a moment and then rose and left the hotel. There was no sign of her anywhere. He wondered whether she had really reported him to Daviot. If she did, it would prove she had nothing to fear.

Hamish walked around the old town all that day under the shadow of the ancient walls, along narrow cobbled streets, across handsome squares while the wind from the Baltic stiffened and ruffled his red hair. Nowhere could he see any sign of Brenda. At last, he returned to her hotel, thinking that as he was in trouble anyway, he might as well try to have another word with her. But he was told at the hotel that she had checked out.

There was nothing more he could do but take the long road home.

On Monday morning, he brushed his uniform before putting it on, polished his boots, and drove to Strathbane to face Daviot.

Detective Chief Inspector Blair was back on duty and grinned when he saw Hamish. "There you are, laddie," he crowed. "And deep, deep in the doo-doo."

He went off laughing as Hamish took the lift up to the top floor. Secretary Helen gave him a thin smile and told him to wait. If he fires me, thought Hamish gloomily, Dick will be left to police my beat and I will lose my home.

At last he was ushered in. He stood nervously in

front of Daviot's desk while the superintendent signed some papers. Then Daviot finally looked up.

"This is a bad business, Macbeth," he said in the quiet voice he used when he was really furious. "I told you to leave Gilchrist alone and you take an unauthorised trip abroad to pester his wife. I have been lenient with you in the past, too lenient. But this is simply too much. You're fired."

In Hamish's mind, his police station, sheep, hens, pets, all whirled away in a black mist. He'd had an uneasy feeling that, in reporting his visit to Estonia, it might mean Brenda had nothing to fear... and yet...

"You should realise, sir, that I must have had a good reason."

"Really? Out with it!"

"It's like this, sir... May I sit down?"

"No."

"It iss verra odd," said Hamish, his highland accent strengthened by his nervousness, "that Mrs. Gilchrist has been travelling for a long time. When I approached her, I could swear she was frightened. Why? Don't you think she might at least have been curious instead of telling me to get lost? Only people with something to hide send the police packing. There have been three murders and I have to look for anything at all that does not fit. And instead of reporting me, you would think that Mr. Gilchrist would want to do his utmost in helping the police instead of blocking us at every turn. The reason the staff at the factory won't say anything, I am sure, is because they have been told not to and have been threatened with losing their jobs. Surely every penny should be going into the factory and not paying for the boss's wife's unlimited travel."

"I happen to know," said Daviot frostily, "that Mrs. Gilchrist is a very wealthy woman in her own right."

"Where does her money come from?"

"Camford Dog Food. When her parents died, she, her sister, Heather, and her brother, Luke, sold the business for a great sum of money. Now, if that is all..."

"Look, sir," said Hamish, "if you take me out of the investigation, you won't get anywhere. I know how the locals think. Give me a little more time and I am sure I can get one of them to talk. I solved the wheelchair murder. I am not stupid. Have my past successes nothing to say for me?"

"Mr. Blair is perfectly competent to head the investigation."

"Mr. Blair is a member of your lodge. That means he is friendly with Mr. Gilchrist. That means that no one will talk to him, least of all Mr. Gilchrist."

Daviot sat scowling. He had to admit that Strathbane police were enduring a lot of criticism in the press over the unsolved murders. He also had to admit in all honesty that Macbeth's quirky and unusual ways had produced dramatic results in the past. Besides, his wife was determined to cultivate a friendship with Priscilla Halburton-Smythe and had hopes that her engagement to Hamish might be on again.

"All right," he said finally. "I will give you one more chance. But be discreet. Keep away from Gilchrist until you have any proof of actual wrongdoing, and I mean concrete proof."

"What was Brenda Gilchrist's maiden name?" asked Hamish.

"Camford, like the dog food," said Daviot reluctantly.

When Hamish returned to the police station, he could hear Dick singing hoarsely above the hum of the new Dyson vacuum cleaner which he had won on a television quiz—*Have You a Clue?* Hamish felt a stab of irritation. It should be a wife he was coming home to, not some fat, lazy policeman.

He shouted at Dick to switch off the vacuum and told him that they had to go out and research the background of Brenda Gilchrist, her brother, and sister.

"Why?" asked Dick plaintively.

"Because I've got a hunch there's something wrong."

"I've just heard the shipping forecast," said Dick.

"What's that got to do with anything?"

"We're to be hit by the tail end of an American

hurricane later today. There's a red alert. Don't drive unless you have to."

"Dick, it blows like hell most of the time in Sutherland. Get your uniform on."

The wind was howling dismally and ruffling the black waters of the loch in Cnothan when they parked outside the factory. The winds of Sutherland usually started with this howling sound which then rose to an eldritch screech and then rose even higher to a peculiar banging sound as if the rain clouds were colliding.

"Going to be bad," muttered Dick. "Who are we going to talk to?"

Hamish glanced at his watch and then reversed the Land Rover until it was outside the Loaming. "Maisie Moffat will be along soon. If we can get her aside and buy her a few drinks, we might get some background on Brenda."

"Why don't we ask that odd job man who takes her to the airport?"

"Maybe later."

They parked and entered the pub. Hamish bagged a corner table. Dick went over to a blackboard to see what was on order for lunch. "What do you want?" he called over one chubby shoulder. "They've got lasagne and chips today."

"Nothing. Just a tonic water," said Hamish.

Dick came back to join him, carrying the tonic

water for Hamish and a half-pint of lager for himself.

Dick's lasagne arrived after ten minutes. "That actually looks good," said Hamish, surprised.

"They get a tray of it from the Italian restaurant in Lochdubh," said Dick. "Do you think Sonsie and Lugs will be all right?"

"They'll be fine," said Hamish. "They're probably along at the kitchen door of the Italian restaurant, cadging food. Here's Maisie."

Maisie had just entered with several other members of the staff. Hamish rose and went to meet her. Dick saw him talking to her and then she followed him reluctantly to join Dick.

"Dick, get Miss Moffat a large vodka and Red Bull," said Hamish.

When Dick went to the bar, Hamish said, "All I want is a bit of background on Brenda Gilchrist."

"Oh, her? She back yet?"

"No, but did she always travel like this?"

"Only this year. She was more o' a Women's Institute type. Good works if it meant she could boss people."

"Where did she come from?"

"I didnae ken. But she was Camford Dog Food. The factory was down in Inverness. Ta." She took the drink Dick was offering her and took a great gulp.

"Did you ever meet her sister?"

"Came up once or twice. Didn't lower herself to speak to the staff. Just looked around the place."

"And the brother, Luke?"

"Never saw him."

"Dick, get Miss Moffat another drink."

Dick cast a fulminating look at his cooling lasagne and stumped up to the bar.

"I'd appreciate it," said Hamish, "if you did not tell anyone what I was asking about."

"I wouldnae dare," said Maisie. "I can tell you that if Mr. Gilchrist heard I'd be out o' a job."

"So why are you talking to me?"

She grinned, taking her fresh drink from Dick. "'Cos I knew you'd get me a drink and I can usually only afford to order a shandy at lunchtime. Go doon tae Inverness and ask the dog food people. They'd know more about the family than me."

"We shouldn't be doing this," grumbled Dick as Hamish took the road to Inverness under an increasingly black sky. "What if the Inverness police see us?"

"I looked up the dog food place. It's actually outside Inverness on the Black Isle."

"The Black Isle's flat," said Dick gloomily.

"What's that got to do with anything?"

"We'll be blown over."

"Havers!"

*   *   *

Meanwhile, Geordie Fleming had not gone for lunch. Instead he had gone home to put another dose of poison at the roots of the monkey puzzle. He had tried again to get permission to cut it down and had once more been turned down. Geordie had heard the dire weather forecast so he poured a lot of poison down on the left-hand side of the tree. The wind would blow fiercely from the west and with any luck, the weakened roots would send the tree toppling over sideways so it would not hit the house. The top of the tree was already swaying in the screeching gale.

He hated that tree with a passion. Because of it blocking light from the house, he had to burn electric light during the day, even in summer.

As Hamish drove into the Black Isle, the Land Rover bucked and swayed dangerously.

The Black Isle is not an island but a peninsula, surrounded on three sides by water: the Cromarty Firth on the north, the Beauly Firth to the south, and the Moray Firth to the east. It got its name because snow was supposed never to lie on it.

Hamish found the industrial site outside Conan Bridge. He parked in the lee of one of the dog food factory's buildings. He and Dick walked round to the reception area at the front, bending before the wind, hanging on to their caps.

They asked to see the manager and were told by a

small man in a brown overall that Mr. Frith would be with them shortly.

Mr. Frith was just as small as his receptionist, a stocky man just under five feet tall with piercing, elongated bright green eyes. It was, thought Hamish, as if the factory were staffed by elves.

"You've just caught me," he said. "I was about to send the staff home. We're in for a bad one."

"I know," said Dick. "I've been trying to tell my sergeant that."

Hamish ignored him. "I wanted to know a bit about the Camford family who used to own this factory."

"You'll need to ask them."

"Where do they live?"

"Cromarty. It's a big Georgian house in the centre of the town called Gateside. The father used his family name for the dog food, and the new owners kept calling it that."

"Cromarty!" panted Dick, nearly breathless from the buffeting of the wind which had struck them, full force, as they had left the reception office. "It's too far in this weather." He fastened his seat belt and looked hopefully at Hamish.

"We're going," said Hamish. "I haven't come all this way to give up."

Dick could only thank his stars that the Black Isle was not blessed with too many trees. As it was,

Hamish had to swerve several times to avoid debris on the road.

Hamish had been born in Cromarty, but his parents had moved to Rogart over near Golspie when he was small.

When they reached the house, a rowan tree had blown down and was blocking the drive.

A thin man was tugging ineffectually at the branches of the fallen tree. "Where can I find Mr. Camford?" shouted Hamish above the screaming wind.

"That's me. What's up? Come into the house."

They followed him into a dim, stone-flagged hallway and then into a sitting room furnished with a Chesterfield sofa and two easy chairs. Dim oil paintings were hung on two walls. The third wall was covered with an old-fashioned glass-fronted bookcase full of leather-bound books which looked as if they had not been read since the eighteenth century. A coal fire sent out puffs of smoke. The room was cold and smelled of damp.

"It's just a routine enquiry," said Hamish. "We're still in the process of excluding people from our enquiries. When your sister Brenda married Harry Gilchrist, did she put much money into the dress factory?"

"He thought she was going to. But she wanted the money for herself. She said she believed in men standing on their own feet. Bit of a letdown for old Harry. But he's made a go of it. Brenda got the bulk of the money, you know. Father left the factory to her and not much to me and Heather. I asked her for some to help modernise this place a bit but she refused. Now, I gather, she does nothing but travel."

"Where can I find your sister Heather?"

"She's travelling as well. Went off with Brenda. I get a postcard from time to time. I wish she'd get back. I don't care if the housing market is low. I'd really like to get rid of this place."

Hamish walked over to a table by the window which contained framed photographs. He picked up one of them, recognising the woman he had spoken to in Tallinn. Beside her was a woman he assumed was Heather. "Your sisters?"

"Yes."

"May I keep this?"

"What … ?"

But before he could finish, there came an almighty crash from over their heads, and rubble and soot fell down the chimney. Luke Camford ran outside. Hamish tucked the photograph into his capacious oilskin pocket and then they followed him.

"A chimney's gone through the upstairs," he shouted. He pulled out his mobile. "I'd better get the fire brigade. Damn. No signal. You're the police. Do something!"

"Are we going to the fire station?" asked Dick as they drove off.

"No. He'll need to fend for himself. I don't want to advertise our presence more than necessary."

Geordie Fleming had not allowed for the fact that if you live in a place with a high dam at one end of the loch and mountains and gully on the other side, then where you live becomes a victim of cross-winds. The tree was beginning to creak and sway alarmingly. He phoned the office and said he was not feeling well. He wanted to be on hand for his triumph when the beastly thing blew down.

"Where's Fleming?" demanded Pete Eskdale. "The boss is shouting for him."

"Haven't seen him," said the secretary, a small girl with hair as ginger as Pete's. "We should all be allowed to go home. There are reports of damage all over the village."

"I'll ask around," said Pete.

He had just left when she received the phone call from Geordie saying he was ill. Gilchrist was somewhere about the factory. She went in search of him, telling everyone she came across to tell the boss that Geordie was at home, sick.

Geordie sat at his living room window amid the horrendous tumult of the storm, watching the tree as it bent and swayed. He began to notice uneasily that the howling wind was switching from east to west and then to the north as it was channelled down the gullies of the mountains opposite.

He decided to go into the kitchen and fix himself a strong drink.

He was just reaching up to the cupboard where he kept a bottle of whisky when, in the roar of the storm, he heard an almighty crack. He swung round in alarm just as the whole tree came crashing down, through the roof and right on top of him, smashing him to the floor in a welter of jagged leaves.

He lost consciousness as pain racked his body. When he recovered his senses he saw that his mobile phone had fallen out of his shirt pocket and was lying a few inches away. He tried to reach it and howled in pain. His arm was broken.

He heard footsteps somewhere in the kitchen and feebly cried, "Help!"

To his horror, the footsteps retreated and he passed out again. Blood from a gash on the back of his head seeped out onto the floor. He briefly came back to consciousness again and muttered one more feeble cry of "Help" before his life ebbed away.

Dick and Hamish took a long time to get back to Lochdubh. Fallen trees and rubble from crashing chimneys had blocked a lot of the way, forcing them to make long detours.

As they headed down the hill to Lochdubh, the storm had rolled away to the east and all that was left was the stormy waves on the loch and knots of villagers, peering anxiously up at their roofs, looking for damage.

Hamish parked in front of the police station and got out. The hill at the end of the village, rising up to the cliffs, had mostly sheltered the station and he was relieved to see there was no sign of any damage.

He went in to the station to a welcome from his pets. The phone in the office was ringing shrilly.

When he picked up the phone, Blair's gloating voice came down the line. "You can go back to your sheep, laddie. We've got our murderer."

"What! Who?"

"Geordie Fleming, that's who."

"That's ridiculous. He wouldnae kill his own sister."

"Got his confession." And infuriatingly, Blair rang off.

Hamish cursed and phoned Jimmy.

"What the hell is this about Geordie Fleming being a murderer?"

"It's right weird," said Jimmy. "Forensics are still investigating. Thon big tree in his garden crashed through the roof and killed him. He'd left a typed confession on his computer."

"For heaven's sakes, man. Anyone could have done that. What did it say?"

"I'll fax you over a copy. Stand by."

Dick walked into the office while Hamish was waiting by the fax machine. "What's up?"

Hamish told him. "Oh, well, that's that," said Dick cheerfully, imagining a return to lazy days.

"I don't believe a word of it," said Hamish furiously. "The man was as meek as a mouse and he wouldnae kill his own sister."

"Did he confess?"

"That great tree in his garden crashed through the roof and killed him. He left a written confession on his computer."

"There you are then."

"There, nothing. Anyone could have written it. They've all gone mad."

The fax machine sprang into life. It spewed out one sheet of paper.

Hamish read: "I, Geordie Fleming, am responsible for the deaths of Morag Merrilea, Fergus McQueen, and my own sister. Morag said I was the father of her child so I had to get rid of her. Fergus was blackmailing me. Hannah knew it was me and said she was going to tell the police. I am very sorry."

"And that's all?" raged Hamish. He sat down at his computer and switched it on. He began to scroll through alibis. It was hard to pinpoint when exactly Morag and Fergus had been killed. No one had thought to question Geordie about his whereabouts when Hannah was killed at the hospital.

Hamish picked up the phone, dialled the factory, and asked to speak to Maisie Moffat. When she came on the line, he said, "I have just heard the news that they are saying Geordie Fleming is the murderer. Do you remember where he was, say, the first time Hannah was attacked and I found her body on the Struie Pass?"

"Wait a bit. Let me think."

There was a long silence while Hamish fretted and chewed his thumbnail.

Then she said, "Well, that's funny."

"What is?"

"I 'member that day. He was in his office, I'll swear, sitting by the phone wi' a face like clay, waiting to see if she phoned."

"I'll be right over for your statement," said Hamish.

Chapter Nine

Leaving Dick behind, Hamish raced over to Cnothan and, ignoring the receptionist, ran up the stairs to where Maisie was waiting. A thin, nervous girl with thick glasses was waiting beside her.

"I got better for ye," crowed Maisie. "This here is Sarah McGowan. Herself was Geordie's secretary. She stuck with him all that time until Hannah was found up on the Struie. And what's mair, himself was at his home, ready to set out for the hospital the day his sister was killt."

Superintendent Daviot gave himself a last glance in the mirror before descending to meet the press who had gathered in front of police headquarters. He had applied a discreet amount of fake tan to his face and felt he was looking at his best.

He was just walking up to a microphone which had been set up on the steps when Jimmy came hurrying up and whispered in his ear.

"Are you sure?" asked Daviot desperately. "But Blair said..."

"Well, Blair was wrong," hissed Jimmy. "Just tell them about the unfortunate death of Geordie and say you're looking into it."

Miserably, Daviot cleared his throat. "Ladies and gentlemen," he began. "I am here to announce the unfortunate death of Geordie Fleming who was killed when a tree in his garden crashed through his house."

Outraged cries sounded in his ears, voices crying that a report had been sent out to the media saying that Geordie Fleming was a murderer and had confessed.

"We are looking into that," said Daviot repressively and turned on his heel and hurried indoors.

"Get over to that factory and see what Macbeth is up to," he said to Jimmy. "And send Blair to my office. And take some men with you and get everyone interviewed all over again."

"Daviot won't thank you for this," said Jimmy when he caught Hamish leaving the factory.

"Did forensic no' check Geordie's computer for prints?" asked Hamish.

"Wiped clean."

"What a bunch of cloth-headed numpties," said Hamish. "Did that not make you just a wee bit suspicious?"

"Man, Blair was all over the place. I couldn't get near the evidence until now."

"Let's go somewhere quiet," begged Hamish. "We've got to talk about this."

"Wait here until I give my men their instructions."

So Hamish waited. It was a balmy day with a pale sun shining through wisps of cloud. It was as if the dreadful storm had never happened.

At last, Jimmy came back to join him.

"Pub," he said. "You're driving." He climbed into the Land Rover.

"Where are your beasties?"

"With Dick Fraser."

"Well, I must say it's grand not to feel their hot breath on the back of my neck."

Once in the pub in the High Street, they settled down at a table in a corner. Jimmy ordered a double whisky for himself and a tomato juice for Hamish.

"This is some amateur as I've said before," said Hamish. "Our killer happened to come by and saw the tree and found Geordie dying and thought of a way to put suspicion on Geordie. I swear we'd have a better chance of getting hold of a professional killer than this lucky sod who blunders around knocking off people. What's behind it? Sex? Money? Have the books been properly audited?"

"Gone through thoroughly. Despite what they claim, the factory was running at a loss, but Gilchrist's wife put a big lump of money into the place."

"When?"

"Must ha' been a couple of months ago."

"Wait a bit. I saw Brenda Gilchrist's brother and he said she refused to give her husband any money and told him he had to stand on his own feet. I went to Estonia to see her."

"You what? If Daviot hears that one, and I'm sure he will, you're toast."

"He has and I nearly got fired over it. There's more. The brother, Luke, he said sister Heather was travelling with her but Brenda was on her own. And Sean Carmichael, Gilchrist's odd job man, said he took Brenda to the airport when she started on her travels. He didn't say anything about Heather."

"What are you on about?"

"What if the woman I saw was Heather Camford, masquerading as her sister?"

"Why?"

"Say Harry Gilchrist needed money for his factory and the wife wouldn't give it, but Heather would in exchange for her sister's money. Brenda got the bulk of the inheritance."

"But why get rid of Morag? Surely if Morag had known anything, she would have told you she suspected Gilchrist."

"Maybe, unless she told Gilchrist that the baby was his. Maybe he stood to lose his respectable name and his factory as well. He was supposed to be in Glasgow on the day Hannah was first attacked. Was that properly checked?"

Jimmy flipped open a briefcase, took out an expensive-looking iPad, and began to search. At last he said, "Here we are. Stayed with a certain Jock Anstruther in Hyndland Road. I've got his number. I'll go outside and phone him."

Hamish waited impatiently.

Jimmy came back, shaking his head. "No, he sticks to his story. He's a director of Anstruther Fabrics."

"I'd like to see him face-to-face," said Hamish. "And we should haul in Sean Carmichael for questioning and then we should get a search warrant for Gilchrist's place and..."

"Wait a minute!" said Jimmy. "Who's in charge of this case? You or me? We won't get a search warrant without proof. We can't go treading on the toes of Strathclyde police. But we will start with Sean...What do you want?"

Stolly Maguire was standing by the table. "I jist wanted tae see if you wanted any mair drinks."

"We don't," snapped Jimmy. "Push off!" He turned

his attention back to Hamish. "Look! All you've got is some pretty mad speculation."

"Humour me," said Hamish. "Let's start off with Sean."

They drove to the Gilchrists' villa but there was no sign of Sean. "Daviot's not going to like this," said Jimmy, "but we're going to have to ask Gilchrist where Sean is."

They were kept waiting at the factory. They were told Mr. Gilchrist was busy.

At last they were ushered in. Gilchrist peered at papers on his desk and, without looking up, said, "How can I help you?"

"We would like to speak to Sean Carmichael," said Jimmy.

"That will not be possible."

"Why?"

"He has just left on a much-needed holiday."

"To where?" demanded Hamish.

"I do not concern myself with the holiday arrangements of the hired help," said Gilchrist, looking up at last.

Jimmy took out his mobile and phoned headquarters. "Put out an alert for Sean Carmichael, all airports, ports, bus stations, train stations, the lot. Appearance?" He handed the phone to Hamish, who rattled off a description.

"Does he have a car?" Hamish asked Gilchrist.

"Yes, an old Ford Escort."

"Do you know the registration number?"

"No, I do not! What is this...?"

"It's an old Ford Escort," said Hamish into the phone. He looked at Gilchrist. "Colour?"

"Red, but..."

"Red," instructed Hamish.

"Get out of here!" raged Gilchrist. "I am going to complain to Mr. Daviot."

"What about?" asked Hamish mildly. "You haven't even asked us why we want to talk to Sean."

"Get out. Out! Out! Out!"

As they left his office, Hamish stopped by the secretary's desk. "Give us Sean Carmichael's address," he ordered.

She looked flustered and glanced nervously at her boss's closed office door.

"Now!" said Jimmy.

She scrolled through her computer, wrote an address on a piece of paper, and handed it to them.

Sean evidently lived in the caravan park just outside Cnothan.

Outside the factory, Jimmy phoned for a search warrant, saying it had to be brought as fast as possible to the caravan park.

*   *   *

The caravan park had a new owner since Hamish had last been there. His name was Gareth Jones, a small, dark Welshman. He said that Sean rented a caravan from him and he could let them in without waiting for the search warrant, as it was his property.

"Have you the registration of his car?" asked Hamish.

"Yes. I'll get it for you. I always write down the registrations in case they run off without paying."

Jimmy took a note of the registration and phoned it over to headquarters. Then they followed Gareth to Sean's caravan, which stood at the end of the park.

The key would not turn in the lock, and a metal bar and padlock had been placed across the door. "That shouldn't be there," raged Gareth.

"Have you bolt cutters?" asked Hamish.

"Yes, I'll get them."

"And bring a crowbar."

"I hope to God there's something incriminating in there," said Jimmy, "before Daviot gets on our back and Blair comes roaring up."

Gareth came back with the bolt cutters. He cut the padlock and took down the metal bar. Then he inserted the crowbar in the doorjamb and wrenched until the door sprang open.

Jimmy went in first, wrinkling his nose. "What a pong! The wee beast probably never washed."

The caravan consisted of two sofas at either side of a table at one end and a bed at the other. In the middle was a small kitchen unit and stove. The aluminum sink was piled high with greasy dishes. Beside the kitchen unit was a wardrobe with drawers underneath. Jimmy and Hamish both put on latex gloves and began to search.

They worked in silence until Jimmy said in disgust, "Nothing but dirty clothes and sheets."

Hamish lifted a strip of carpet from the floor. Underneath was a trapdoor. He lifted it up, and, getting down on his knees, pulled out a metal box. "Padlocked," he said. "I'll see if Gareth is still out there with the bolt cutters."

Gareth was nowhere to be seen, but the bolt cutters were propped against the door.

Hamish carried them in and cut the padlock. Jimmy crouched down beside him as Hamish opened the lid.

"Would ye look at that?" breathed Jimmy.

The box was stuffed with colourful Bank of Scotland notes. Sir Walter Scott's face in blue, brown, purple, green, and red stared up at them. The hundred-pound notes were red, and there were more of them than any of the lower denominations.

"I'll count them out," said Jimmy. "Get Gareth here. We need a witness."

When Gareth arrived, the Welshman stared at the money. "I want you to witness what we've got here," said Jimmy. "Don't want any accusations that the police put any of this in their pockets."

"And when you've counted it," said Hamish, "put it back."

"Why?" said Jimmy. "Five thousand and five. Damn, I think I've lost count."

"Don't you see," said Hamish, "he must have left in a rush. His clothes are all here. He must have got a tip-off and fled from the Gilchrists' villa. He'll try to come back for this."

"He'll see the door smashed," said Jimmy, sitting back on his heels, "and run for his life."

"Aye, but if we keep watch, we could nab him before he gets near the caravan."

"Why all this money?" asked Jimmy.

"I think maybe someone was paying him to keep quiet—or maybe for some nasty work he did," said Hamish. "I think it should be just us two that waits for him. You bring in a lot of men and it might fall to pieces. A strange face stands out a mile in this place. He may have friends in one of the other caravans."

"Gareth," asked Jimmy, "does the wee swine have friends here?"

"No, he kept himself to himself."

"I still think it should be the two of us," said Hamish, "and don't report to Blair or he'll come charging up here."

"The tourists have all gone," said Gareth. "There was one nasty type called Box but he left just after I took over. I've only got the one couple at the moment.

They're down in Glasgow at the moment, visiting relatives, so you've got the place to yourselves."

To Jimmy's relief, there was no phone call from Blair. Blair was down at police headquarters, swearing blind that Geordie was the real murderer and everything else was just a waste of time.

Fortunately for them, the long summer was over and darkness was falling earlier. But by two in the morning, both Jimmy and Hamish were tired and hungry. The caravan park was up on a hill above the village. Looking down, they could see the whole place was as quiet as the grave.

They were crouched behind a gorse bush. "The ground's damp," whispered Jimmy. "I'm getting up to stretch my legs."

He half rose but Hamish pulled him down. "Listen!"

"I don't hear a car."

"I heard a twig snap. I think he's coming over the back on foot."

"I cannae hear anything."

"Shh!"

The light from a pencil torch suddenly stabbed through the darkness.

They waited until, in the starlight, they saw a silhouette against the caravan.

Jimmy rushed forward. "Sean Carmichael. I am Detective Jimmy Anderson and I am..."

That was as far as he got. Sean turned and ran up the bray. Hamish brought him down with a rugby tackle and then handcuffed him. Jimmy called for two policemen to come and guard the caravan and the money. When they finally arrived, Jimmy went to get the Land Rover. Sean, who maintained a sullen silence, was thrust in the back and then, with Hamish driving and Jimmy following in his unmarked car, they set out for police headquarters.

It was agreed to interview Sean in the morning after they had both got a few hours' sleep.

Hamish took a bed in the sickroom and fell immediately asleep without bothering to undress.

He was awakened roughly in the morning by Jimmy. "Get up, man. The wee bugger's topped himself."

"He can't have!" exclaimed Hamish, struggling awake. "Didn't the custody sergeant take away his belt and shoelaces?"

"Aye, but he didnae take away what Sean said were his high blood pressure pills. They were in the right sort of box wi' the pharmacist's label and all. Some sort of lethal drug. Won't know till the autopsy. Daviot's in and wants to see us."

"Sir," said Hamish, after they had given their report to Daviot, "we'll need a search warrant for Gilchrist's house. And he should be brought in for questioning immediately."

"I cannot see what a respectable man like Harry Gilchrist has got to do with any of this," said Daviot.

"Sean was working for him," said Jimmy patiently. "He had that box full of money. Okay, suppose Gilchrist is innocent. We still need to ask him all he knows about Sean."

"We need to use tact here. I'll send Mr. Blair."

"But, sir...," began Jimmy.

"No, those are my orders. Macbeth, I suggest you get a shave. And there are bits of bush sticking to your sweater."

"That's blown it," said Hamish as he wearily took his leave of Jimmy after typing out a long report of the arrest of Sean Carmichael. "Blair crawls to folk like Gilchrist. He'll toddle back to Daviot with a report that the man is as pure as the snow on the top o' Ben Nevis."

Hamish drove wearily back to the police station. He was welcomed at the kitchen door by Dick. "Where were you?" asked Dick. "You might have phoned. I was worried about you."

"Get out of my way," said Hamish crossly. "We're not married."

But as he slumped down at the kitchen table, he mumbled thanks as Dick put a cup of his excellent coffee in front of him. Hamish roused himself to tell Dick what had been happening.

"They should ha' got that search warrant," said Dick. "Mark my words, Gilchrist will make a run for it."

"So you think he's guilty?"

"Of course," said Dick, leaning one fat hip against the kitchen counter. "Iffy stuff about the wife, his creature Sean kills himself, he's bound to be behind it all."

"Damn Daviot and his cronies," said Hamish. "It seems that all a murderer needs is a veneer of respectability and a membership of the Strathbane Lodge to be thought innocent."

The phone in the office rang. Hamish went to answer it. Jimmy's agitated voice came down the line. "No one can find Gilchrist. He hasn't been at work today. Daviot's cracked and is getting a search warrant."

"I'm coming over right away," said Hamish. He went back to the kitchen. "Get your uniform on, Dick. We're getting a search warrant for Gilchrist's home."

Nessie and Jessie Currie turned on the waterfront to watch the police Land Rover racing off out of the village.

"Our lazy policeman seems to be working at last," said Nessie, and then, ignoring the echoing voice of her sister, she said uneasily, "I shouldnae have reported that business about him spending the night wi'

Hannah Fleming to his bosses. He hasnae spoken to me since."

"It was a spiteful thing to do," said her twin. "I always thought so."

"You didnae say anything at the time."

And, quarrelling, they made their way to Patel's grocery store.

"Where's Blair?" asked Hamish when they arrived at Gilchrist's villa.

"After he phoned Daviot with the bad news, he went to the Loaming for a refresher, tripped on the doorstep, came down like a ton o' bricks."

"Some good news anyway," said Hamish heartlessly.

An unmarked car drove up and Daviot climbed out. "I have the search warrant," he said.

"Right," said Jimmy. He shouted to three policemen standing by the door of the villa, "Go ahead."

One policeman took out his truncheon and smashed the stained-glass panel on the front door, reached inside, and unlocked it.

"Come on, Hamish," said Jimmy. "Let's see if the bastard is inside."

"Perhaps the forensic team should go in first," said Daviot.

"We'll let them in if he's not there," said Jimmy.

Hamish and Jimmy drew on latex gloves and entered the shadowy hall, picking their way gingerly over broken shards of glass. Jimmy pushed open a door off the hall. "This is his office," he said. "I'll go through the papers while you and the men make sure he's not at home."

While police fanned out through the house, Hamish stood in the hall looking around.

"I wonder if this place has a basement," he murmured.

At the back of the hall, he found a stout wooden door, heavily padlocked.

He went outside. Dick was sitting in a canvas chair on the drive with the dog and cat at his feet.

"Get me bolt cutters," shouted Hamish.

When Dick had produced the bolt cutters from the back of the Land Rover, Hamish went back into the house and cut the padlock on the basement door.

He found a light switch and turned it on. Steep stone steps led downwards.

There was nothing in the basement but one large cabin trunk. Hamish smashed the lock with the bolt cutters and swung back the lid. It was full of women's clothes, shoes, and underwear. He carefully searched through the contents.

Then he turned and looked around. The floor was flat, even cement. The walls were brick. But one wall over on the right had new bricks in it.

Hamish took out a stout clasp knife and scraped

away at the plaster around one of the bricks. It had been an amateur job of bricklaying, for the brick came out easily. He prised out another and another until he had made a square hole. A ghastly sweetish smell was emanating from the hole. He unclipped a flashlight from his belt and shone it into the aperture. A horrible decomposing face stared back at him.

Hamish backed away.

He sprinted up the stairs and told Jimmy what he had found. Jimmy followed him down the stairs.

"If I'm not mistaken," said Hamish, "that will turn out to be Brenda Gilchrist with her own sister masquerading as her somewhere abroad."

Daviot looked appalled at the news. He sent in the forensic team and then said he would hurry back to headquarters to coordinate a search for the missing Gilchrist and contact Interpol to pick up anyone using Brenda Gilchrist's passport.

"What now?" asked Dick.

"We wait and see what more the forensic team comes up with," said Jimmy.

Dick heaved himself out of his chair. "It's a good thing I'm prepared," he said. He heaved a large picnic basket out of the Land Rover. "Something I made earlier," he said with a grin.

Under Jimmy's bemused stare, Dick took out flasks of coffee and wrapped packets of sandwiches.

"That's a right good wife you've got there," said Jimmy.

"Shut up," said Hamish.

"It's shut up, *sir*. Know your place," said Jimmy.

Hamish had that longing again to get his police station back to himself. There should be a woman looking after him, some pretty woman, some wife instead of a middle-aged policeman.

"These are grand sandwiches," said Jimmy. "Got anything to drink?"

"You've got coffee," said Dick.

"I mean a proper drink."

Dick fished in the depths of the basket and produced a bottle of beer.

"Man, you're the best," said Jimmy. "Hamish, you are one lucky man. He's even got your terrifying beasties behaving themselves."

Who will rid me of this domesticated copper? wondered Hamish.

Outside the entrance to the drive and kept at bay by two policemen were the press. It seemed their numbers were growing in size every moment.

"How do they find out so quickly?" marvelled Jimmy.

"Easy," said Hamish. "An all-points bulletin about Gilchrist has probably already been on the radio and flashed on all the television channels."

"The man must be mad," said Jimmy.

"It's loss of respectability," said Hamish. "He's a pillar of the community. Morag probably told him the baby was his. He may have paid Sean to get rid of her."

"But why drug her that time instead of bumping her off?"

"He may have been keeping his wife drugged. Maybe she staggered out and looked in the window of the pub. That was when Morag might have sketched her. Then Morag goes around saying she's going to a hypnotist and that's when Gilchrist took action. Then it all snowballed. He must have been romancing the sister and they both wanted Brenda's money."

"But he couldnae have gone on and on pretending his wife was abroad," protested Jimmy.

"They'd have thought of something. Maybe the fake Brenda could file for divorce claiming to be the guilty party. She settles a sum of money on Gilchrist, waits a bit, he sells the now profitable factory, and the pair of them go off hand in hand into the sunset of some foreign beach. I think she's the mover and shaker behind all this."

"But why would Sean commit suicide? It's not as if we have the death penalty."

"What if...just what if...Sean really had high blood pressure? What if poison was substituted for his regular pills? Think about it. He's under strain after his arrest. So he takes a couple of what he thinks are high blood pressure pills and gets poisoned."

"Well, we'll know when the results of the autopsy come through," said Jimmy. "In the meantime, Hamish, why don't you and Dick go and see the doctor in Cnothan." He consulted his notes. "The pills were prescribed by a Dr. Stanley. The surgery is in the High Street."

Dr. Stanley confirmed that he had prescribed high blood pressure pills for Sean. Hamish and Dick returned to give Jimmy the news.

"Now all we have to do is wait and see if Gilchrist can be found," said Jimmy. He suddenly wanted rid of Hamish before Daviot came back. Blair was getting increasingly accident-prone. Jimmy coveted his job. He didn't want Hamish around stealing his thunder.

"You and Dick had better just go back to Lochdubh," he said. "I'll keep you informed."

"But..."

"That's an order," said Jimmy.

Chapter Ten

He who steals my purse steals trash; 'tis something, nothing;
'Twas mine, 'tis his, and has been slave to thousands;
But he that filches from me my good name
Robs me of that which not enriches him,
And makes me poor indeed.

—William Shakespeare

Hamish sat in the police station office. He leaned back in his chair, his arms behind his head. Where would Gilchrist run to?

And that barman, Stolly, should be brought in for questioning. He was hovering near their table in the pub when they were talking about going to see Sean.

If Gilchrist was tipped off through Stolly, he might go straight to Sean and somehow manage to substitute the poison—if it should turn out to be poison—for the blood pressure pills.

He frowned. He was sure that the woman he'd met

in Tallinn was Heather, and she had been a forceful character. Maybe the mover and shaker. Maybe Sean was paid to do the murders so that Gilchrist would always have the perfect alibi.

He was sure Gilchrist was panicked into it all by the thought of losing his position in the community.

Mairie Torrich had tried to kill herself because she thought she had lost her good name.

What if Gilchrist had fled somewhere to put an end to himself? Where would he go? All the hotels would be checked. Would he go abroad for a last farewell to Heather? But he would know that all the airports would be watched along with the ferries and train stations.

Where would the hunted animal that was Gilchrist go to earth?

He suddenly jumped to his feet, ran out of the police station, and got into the Land Rover.

Down in Glasgow, Elspeth Grant was summoned by her boss, Barry Dalrymple.

"Take a seat, Elspeth," said Barry.

They surveyed each other with the embarrassment of a couple who have once been engaged and shared a bed.

"You've heard what's been happening up in the Highlands?" began Barry.

"Yes, I announced the search for Harry Gilchrist on the midday news."

"It's like this. No one knows that area better than you, and you've got an in with that weird copper, what's his name?"

"Hamish Macbeth."

"Yes, him. We'd like you to go up there and file a report."

Elspeth looked at him cynically. "What bit of totty have you found to replace me while I'm up there?"

"Now, Elspeth, we all know now that Hannah was a mistake. James Garden will fill in for you. You must admit he's no competition. It should only take you a couple of days."

"Oh, all right," conceded Elspeth. "When do I start?"

"What about right now?"

Hamish drove to the small Church of Scotland, St. Andrew's, in Cnothan. He tried the door, but it was locked.

He went to the manse next door. When the minister, John Gordon, opened the door, Hamish said, "I'd like to get into the church. It's urgent."

Mr. Gordon smiled. "We do not take confessions in the Church of Scotland, but if there's anything I can help or advise..."

"I need the key," said Hamish. "Did Harry Gilchrist have a key?"

"Yes, he does. But..."

"I need it now. He may be in there."

Mr. Gordon retreated into the manse and shortly returned with a large key. Hamish seized it and ran into the church, followed by the minister.

He unlocked the door and swung it open.

Thin light shone through the plain glass latticed windows.

"There's no one here," said Mr. Gordon.

Hamish strode down the church, bending down and looking in all the pews. He finally straightened up and looked around.

"The bell," he said. "Where do you ring the bell?"

"It's the room over there on your left, next to the vestry."

Hamish went over and swung open the door. Unlike some other churches, St. Andrew's had only one bell.

Hanging from the bell rope, his face hideously distorted, was Harry Gilchrist.

Behind him, Mr. Gordon exclaimed, "This is horrible. I'll get a knife and we'll cut him down."

"No," said Hamish. "I'm afraid we'll have to wait until the Scenes of Crimes Operatives have gone over the place thoroughly. I'm sure he's committed suicide, but we have to be sure."

The minister retreated to the church, sank down in a pew, and began to pray.

Hamish took out his phone.

*   *   *

An hour later, Hamish, Jimmy, and Daviot waited outside the church while white-coated figures did their business inside. At last, one of them came out and handed Daviot a sealed envelope. "This was in his pocket, sir. It's addressed to you."

Jimmy handed his boss a pair of latex gloves. Daviot put them on and opened the envelope. He read the contents slowly and then handed the letter that was inside to Jimmy.

Hamish crowded forward to read it over his shoulder. "I am sorry," Gilchrist had written. "I never meant to hurt anyone. I leave the factory and all my possessions to my dear wife, Brenda." There was a scrawl of a signature at the bottom.

"Are we sure yet that the woman bricked up is his wife?" asked Daviot. "The results have yet to come through. I mean, all we have at the moment is your speculations, Macbeth. We're waiting for the DNA results."

"There is one way to find out, sir," said Hamish.

"What's that?"

"I'm sure you have already done it," said Hamish who was pretty sure they hadn't. "Freeze all bank accounts and credit cards in the name of Brenda Gilchrist."

"I'm sure Mr. Blair will have seen to that."

"I don't think he'll have been able to," said Jimmy, taking out his phone. "I'll get them on to it right away."

"How on earth did you guess he would come here?" asked Daviot, walking a little way away through the gravestones with Hamish. "I thought I knew him. He and his wife have been to my home for dinner. He seemed a pillar of the community."

"He was suffering from a combination of greed and respectability," said Hamish. "He could not bear the thought of going on trial and the world knowing exactly what he was like. But if Heather is masquerading as his wife, I feel she might have been the one who drove him on."

They turned round as the body was wheeled out of the church. Jimmy had finished his phone call and had talked to the head of the forensics team. "It does seem he topped himself," he said. "That letter is pretty much a confession. But they're still dusting for fingerprints to make sure he was alone."

Daviot turned to Hamish. He felt irritated with this lanky police sergeant. He did not trust Hamish's unorthodox leaps of the imagination and always found it hard to give him credit for anything.

"Get back to your station, Macbeth," he ordered, "and file a full report. Anderson and I will handle the press."

And take all the credit as usual, thought Hamish cynically.

He drove slowly back to Lochdubh. The day was warm. The early frosts had not yet arrived. The landscape dreamt under a benign sun. A stag up on a brae above the road looked down on him.

What a blundering murderer Gilchrist had been— if he had done any of the murders himself. Or had he paid Sean? Well, he supposed he would find out after all the forensic reports were in.

Dick was asleep on a deck chair in the garden, his moustache gently rising and falling as he snored.

Sonsie and Lugs were lying at his feet. They opened their eyes as Hamish looked over the hedge and then went back to sleep. Hamish remembered how not so long ago they would have come running to welcome him.

With a sigh, he went into the station, into his office, switched on the computer, and began to type.

He finished an hour later, collected his pets from the garden, and walked along the waterfront. A thin mist was settling down on the forest trees across the loch. The loch itself was still and quiet. Sounds of clattering dishes and snatches of television reached his ears as Lochdubh prepared for high tea—dinner in most other places.

Hamish saw the Currie sisters approaching and stared fixedly at the loch. From behind him came Nessie's voice.

"I'm right sorry, Hamish."

"Sorry," echoed her sister.

"I should never have reported ye. I don't know what came over me."

I do, you jealous, shrivelled-up old bitch, thought Hamish. You can't bear to think of anyone having it off.

But he turned round and smiled down at her. "That's all right. Let's forget it."

Jessie held out a box. "We brought you some of our scones," said Nessie.

"Scones," said her sister.

The Currie sisters' scones were as light as feathers.

"Thank you," said Hamish, taking the box.

They both bobbed their heads to him and went on their way.

Every time I think of Hannah, I feel vicious with shame, thought Hamish. How could I have fallen for just good looks? But he had done exactly that on his last case. He had nearly become besotted by a certain Mary Leinster who had turned out to be a nasty piece of work.

He turned and walked slowly back to the police station. Dick was in the kitchen, preparing a steak and kidney pie. "I heard the news on the telly," said Dick, rolling pastry. "So that's all wrapped up."

"No, it isn't," said Hamish, putting the box of scones on the table. "We've still to find Heather. We're waiting for the DNA report to make sure that it's definitely her sister we found murdered."

Heather Camford finished a meal in an oyster bar on the Boulevard St. Germain in Paris. She did not watch television and did not know that Interpol was searching for her. She called for the bill and took out one of Brenda's credit cards.

Heather then looked up startled when the waiter said apologetically that the card was not working. She had two more credit cards and two debit cards. She tried them all without success.

"I'll get the manager," said the waiter.

Heather thought quickly. It was a warm evening and she had selected a table on the pavement so she could smoke. She fled down the street, slowing her pace when she reached the bottom of the Rue Dante. She turned along Rue Lagrange and down Rue Maitre Albert to her hotel. She was about to go in when she saw two policemen at the desk.

She hurried on down towards the Seine. What had gone wrong? Hurrying over the bridge, she went into the park below Notre Dame. She took out her mobile phone and tried to call Gilchrist. A man answered. She knew immediately the voice on the other end was not that of Harry Gilchrist. She switched it off.

Heather was possessed of a sort of mulish stupidity allied to greed and arrogance. She could hardly believe they had been found out. She had, however, been clever enough to buy a fake passport and driving licence in Barcelona, and it was on this passport that she had paid a flying visit to Scotland, arriving in time to hear Harry Gilchrist's warning that Hannah Fleming was about to talk. He had given her the name of the hotel. When Hannah had appeared, she had called out, "It's me, Brenda Gilchrist. Want a lift?"

The silly bitch hadn't died and so Harry had to pay Sean to finish the work.

She opened her wallet. She had 450 euros left. With luck, she had hired a car with the fake driving licence. It was in the underground car park in Rue Lagrange. She must get to it and drive... where? Back to Cnothan was the answer. That was the last place they would look for her. She had a key to the factory and knew the code of the burglar alarm. And she also knew the combination to the safe. With enough money, she could disappear again.

Hamish was just finishing his dinner when Jimmy arrived. "There was a cosh thrown in beside the body. It's got Heather's fingerprints on it. They're rushing the DNA, but we're pretty sure that the dead body is Brenda. Has wifie got anything to drink?"

Dick scowled but produced a bottle of whisky and three glasses.

"How could they get away with so much murder and mayhem?" asked Jimmy.

"A combination of cunning, fear, stupidity, and incredible luck," said Hamish. "A clever murderer would never have picked up Hannah at that hotel, fearing CCTV cameras. I think we may have three murderers.

I think Heather killed Brenda and maybe Hannah, Gilchrist killed Fergus and Geordie, and maybe Sean finished off Hannah. What was in Sean's pills?"

"Oblivon. Used by vets. Instant and deadly."

"I thought that was a liquid."

"It is. But the medicine was in capsules. All someone had to do was inject the capsules with the stuff. It takes very little."

Jimmy's phone rang. He listened and then snapped, "Make sure all the ports and airports are watched. And pay special attention to the Eurostar."

When he rang off, he said, "Heather's been spotted in Paris. She tried to use Brenda's cards and when they wouldn't work, she fled."

There was a knock at the kitchen door. Hamish went to answer it and found Elspeth Grant smiling up at him.

"Come ben," said Hamish.

"I'm off," said Jimmy, draining his glass. "I'll keep you posted."

When he had gone, Dick took down an apron from a hook and wrapped it round his generous middle. "Why don't you pair go through to the living room while I clear up."

Elspeth looked around the living room in amazement. A bright fire was burning, the evening having turned cold. Hamish's shabby furniture had been covered with chintz. She noticed the flat-screen television and the latest in stereo equipment.

"Did you win the lottery, Hamish?"

"No, it's Dick. He's a whiz at quizzes and keeps winning prizes."

"I didn't think you could win chintz covers."

"He won a sewing machine and made them himself."

"How domesticated you are! Better than a wife."

"Let's talk about something else. I suppose you've come about the murders. If you write anything, let me see it first."

"Sure. Is the dead body Brenda Gilchrist?"

"Yes, but don't write anything about that until you get the official confirmation."

"Tell me about it all."

So Hamish did, feeling at ease in her company. She was wearing a checked shirt and jeans instead of one of her usual power suits. Because of the dampness of the evening, her hair had begun to frizz, reminding him of how she used to look when she was only a local reporter.

When he had finished, she said in amazement, "It all sounds like blundering from one murder to another."

"That's what held up the investigation," said Hamish. "We were looking first of all for one person and a clever one at that."

"Why did Sean kill himself? He could confess to lying about taking Brenda to the airport and say that his boss paid him to say it. He would have got off on a minor charge."

"I think somehow he was murdered. Poison was substituted for those high blood pressure pills of his. I think maybe Gilchrist planned to get rid of him even before Sean fled. I can't believe he put it there himself. What I'm trying to figure out is what will Heather do next? She hasn't any money. If she wants to stay hidden, she'll need money."

"With her track record, she'll probably just mug someone," said Elspeth.

Heather, having reached London, spent the remainder of the night in her car in the back streets of South London. Then in the morning, she left the car with the keys in the ignition. With any luck someone would steal it.

She took the tube to Trafalgar Square and walked along to the Savoy Hotel where she ordered breakfast. She was wearing a broad-brimmed hat and glasses and had padded out her cheeks. She waited until she saw a wealthy-looking woman rise from the table, say something to her husband, and head for the ladies' room.

She followed. To her relief, there was no woman on duty. Her quarry came out of the toilet, placed her capacious handbag beside one of the sinks, and began to wash her hands. Another woman came in and hailed the first one. "Alice, dear, were you waiting long for us? John's with your husband. How did you get on with...?" Her voice sank to a whisper. Both women glanced at Heather and then moved over to a corner to have a muttered conversation.

Heather quickly zipped open Alice's handbag, extracted her wallet, took out a thick pile of notes, replaced the wallet, and zipped up the handbag again.

She quickly left, walking straight out of the hotel and vanishing into the morning crowds.

When she felt safe, she went into a café and checked the amount. Over five hundred pounds. Silly woman to carry that much cash around with her. She was just asking to be robbed.

She went to a car rental agency and, using her false passport and driving licence, hired a Ford.

Elspeth stood in front of the factory the morning after her evening with Hamish, interviewing members of the staff. Many were in tears. All they could think about was the fact that the business would be closed down and they would lose their jobs.

The best interview was with Freda Crichton. Her fashion show had been cancelled. Elspeth and her cameraman and crew followed Freda into her studio and filmed her designs.

"How could this happen to me?" wailed Freda when the interview was over. "Our wages haven't been paid. They're all in the safe. I feel like breaking into it."

She walked with Elspeth out of the factory and stood blinking in the sunlight. "It seems worse in sunny weather," said Freda. "It ought to be black and stormy."

After she had said goodbye to Freda, her cameraman asked, "What next?"

"Down to the Black Isle and interview Heather's brother," said Elspeth.

As they drove out of Cnothan and headed south, Elspeth took out her phone and called Hamish.

"It's been a miserable morning," she said. "Those poor souls at the factory haven't even been paid their wages. The money's all locked up in the safe."

There was a long silence from Hamish's end of the phone.

"Hamish? Are you still there?"

"Do you know if the late Brenda had keys to the factory and knew the combination to the safe?" asked Hamish.

"I never thought to ask. Why? Heather wouldn't dare to come back."

"Why not?" asked Hamish. "She'll maybe think Cnothan would be the last place anyone would be looking for her and she'll need money."

"It's a long shot."

"I'm going to bed down in that factory and wait and see," said Hamish.

Elspeth said goodbye and rang off. Then she turned

to the cameraman who was driving. "Turn around," she ordered. "We're going back."

Hamish phoned Jimmy and outlined his theory. "It's a long shot," said Jimmy. "But if you want to kip in the factory, it's up to you. I can't see Daviot giving permission."

"Then don't tell anyone," said Hamish. "Who will inherit Heather's money?"

"Nobody. She got it through crime."

"So who inherits Brenda's money? Did she leave a will?"

"Yes, and it's probably what got her killed. She left the lot to her brother, Luke Camford. I'd keep watch with you, Hamish, but to be honest, I think it's a daft idea and there's miles of paperwork to do."

"I'll take Dick."

"Good luck with that one. How will you keep him awake?"

"Do one thing for me," said Hamish. "Get me the code for the burglar alarm and the safe."

Dick accepted Hamish's plan placidly. Like Jimmy, he thought it was a mad idea, but it meant, with any luck, he could just sleep the night away.

Joan Friend, the publicist, phoned Hamish in the afternoon, to say that police had removed all documents from the factory.

"What about the staff's money?" asked Hamish anxiously.

"They'll leave that for the receivers. The staff are planning a protest tomorrow. It's ridiculous. We all need to be paid."

"When were you last paid?" asked Hamish.

"Last month. We're paid monthly."

"But doesn't the money get paid straight into your bank accounts?"

"Gilchrist always kept it in the safe for some reason and then at the end of each month, a security firm came and took it to the bank."

When she rang off, Hamish silently praised the stupidity of the police and the receivers. That money should have been moved to the bank. There must be a small fortune in there.

The same thought had crossed Heather's mind. She stopped on the road north and phoned the factory and asked to be put through to Gilchrist's secretary. Saying she was phoning from police headquarters, she asked if the staff's wages had been removed. Assured they had not, she breathed a sigh of relief. Thank God she had kept the keys to the factory.

Hamish and Dick waited until midnight and then set out, wearing dark clothes. Dick was driving his old car.

The night was still and clear with the black silhouettes of the mountains rearing up against a starry sky. Dick's little car wound its way along the one-track road beneath the vast glory of the Sutherland night sky like some small, dark, insignificant bug.

Cnothan was quiet and silent. Many of the staff had got drunk and were sleeping off the effects.

"What if we're too late?" said Dick as he turned the car along the waterfront.

"She'll wait until everyone has left the pub and went home. She won't want the risk of anyone seeing her," said Hamish.

"What about the burglar alarm?"

"I've got the code."

"What about keys to get in?"

"I have my methods, Watson. No, don't drive up to the factory. Go past it and park up at the end of the road where there aren't any houses. We'll walk back."

When Dick had parked under the spreading branches of a rowan tree, they got out and made their way silently to the factory. "Round the side to the staff door," said Hamish.

He took out a ring of skeleton keys and fiddled with the locks. After ten minutes, he opened the door and quickly switched off the burglar alarm.

Using pencil torches, they crept up the stairs and along corridors to Gilchrist's office.

"What makes you think she'll come tonight?" asked Dick, who was beginning to feel sleepy.

"Then we'll come back tomorrow night," said Hamish. "And the night after that."

"Where do we sit?" asked Dick.

"On the floor, behind the desk."

"Can't I sit in a chair? My knees get stiff."

"No. And if you go to sleep and snore, I'll cosh you!"

They settled down, side by side on the floor.

"Thon Elspeth's a bonny lassie," said Dick. "Ever think of getting married?"

"The whole time," muttered Hamish.

"You're joking, aren't you?" said Dick uneasily.

"Shhh. Don't say another word."

An hour dragged past. Dick, who had been praying before that Heather would not come because he didn't like action, now prayed she would. He knew that if she did not, then stubborn Hamish would come the next night and the night after that. He began to feel stiff and cold and sulky. It was just one of Hamish's mad speculations. Heather had probably got herself to one of those countries where she couldn't be extradited.

Dick closed his eyes and soon he was asleep.

Beside him, Hamish struggled to keep awake. Then he thought he heard a slight noise and nudged Dick awake.

"I heard something," he whispered.

They both sat, straining their ears. Then Hamish

thought he heard soft footsteps coming along the corridor outside.

"Get ready," he said quietly.

The door of the office opened and he stiffened. Then the door closed and the footsteps went away. He could hear doors along the corridor opening and closing and then silence.

"What on earth...?" he muttered.

He looked down from the window and saw black-masked figures outside. Before he could shout, one of them hurled a Molotov cocktail through the downstairs reception windows and another man tossed another.

"My God!" he shouted. "They're burning down the factory!"

He went to the safe and opened it. He looked around wildly for something to put the money in and then saw a travel bag on top of a filing cabinet. He stuffed the money in and zipped up the bag.

"Come on, Dick. They've attacked the front. We may get out the side door."

They hurried along the corridor and down the back stairs. The fire was taking hold. Before they reached the first landing, they could see the red glow below them, and they were beginning to choke with the smoke.

"Back up!" shouted Hamish. "We'll need to try to get out of a back window and climb down."

They rushed back up the stairs and along the corridor to Pete Eskdale's room, which was at the back.

Hamish thrust open the window. "It's three floors down, Dick. We'll need to try to make it."

"I cannae," panted Dick. "I'll never do it."

"There's a drainpipe outside. Follow me."

Hamish tossed the bag down to the ground and swung a leg over the sill. He climbed down a bit and stared up at Dick's anguished face.

"Come on, man! Do you want to burn?"

Dick eased his plump body over the sill and grabbed the drainpipe. Hand over hand they made their way down.

Dick fell the last few feet and crashed into Hamish.

"You nearly broke my bones," grumbled Hamish. "Are you all right?"

"Bit winded," gasped Dick.

"Round to the front and see if we can catch some of the bastards."

But in the red glow from the burning building, they could see no one around.

Hamish took out his phone and called headquarters and was told that it had already been reported and the fire engines and police were on their way.

"Let's get this money back to the car and lock it in the boot."

They walked along to where they had parked the car. "Let the police look for the culprits," said Hamish.

"They're bound to get them. Cnothan's a small place and they'll do a house-to-house search."

"They'll need search warrants," said Dick, "or they'll go tae the European Court of Human Rights."

Hamish told the night sky that the Court of Human Rights could go and perform an impossible anatomical act upon itself as Dick unlocked the boot.

"I'll take that," said a woman's voice.

Hamish turned round. A tall woman he was sure was Heather was standing there, starlight glinting on the deadly-looking gun she held in her hand.

"Heather Camford," said Hamish bleakly. "There's nothing but my dirty clothes in the bag."

"I'll take that risk. Throw it over."

Hamish could hear the approaching wail of sirens. To his horror, Dick walked calmly in front of him and said, "You're not getting the bag."

"I'll shoot you!"

"Go ahead," said Dick.

She screamed in fury, threw the gun at him, and began to run towards the burning building. Hamish raced after her as she headed straight for the flames.

Dick cannoned into Hamish and knocked him to the ground. "Let the bitch burn!" he panted.

Hamish struggled to his feet. He hurtled after Heather and reached her just as her clothes caught fire. As the fire brigade arrived, he rolled her on the ground. She was screaming in agony, and half her face was badly burned.

Fortunately an ambulance arrived at the same time and Hamish shouted at them to give her a shot of something.

When Heather was sedated, Jimmy arrived and Hamish briefly told him what had happened. "I'll go with her to the hospital," said Jimmy. "You send a report. I've got men arriving to go round the village and see who set this place alight. Or was it her?"

He suddenly turned and yelled, "Turn that camera off!" Elspeth had arrived with her crew.

"No," said Hamish, "we looked down from the building and saw about five of them with masks on."

Jimmy got in the ambulance, and it drove off as the firemen began to shoot water into the building.

Elspeth came running up to Hamish, but he said sharply, "Not now. Call on me tomorrow." He and Dick walked away.

"Your clothes are a bit scorched," said Dick. "Why on earth didn't you let her burn?"

"I didn't want her to escape justice. All I could think of were the lives she had ruined. We'd better get a couple of policemen to check the money in the bag so we can't be accused of taking any. Then we'd better take the lot to Strathbane. Dick, you tried to save my life. I'll never understand why she didn't just shoot us."

"I recognised a replica, even in the dark," said Dick. "I make a study o' a lot of things for my quizzes."

Hamish began to laugh and was still laughing while Dick went to fetch a couple of policemen as witnesses.

They were exhausted when they arrived at Strathbane. Daviot, looking unusually rumpled because he had been called out from his bed, congratulated them. He led them upstairs to his office, and the bag and the witness statements were put into his safe.

Hamish wearily told him all about their adventures.

When he had finished, Daviot said, "When you heard those footsteps, did you think it was her?"

Hamish shook his head. "I think it was one of the arsonists, checking to make sure no one was in the building. I suppose there's usually a night watchman. Oh, it makes me sick. I know they shouldnae ha' burned the factory, but now they won't only be poor, they'll all have criminal records."

"You did good work," said Daviot, but wishing, not for the first time, that Hamish Macbeth was not so ... well ... unconventional in his methods.

"Will she live?" asked Hamish.

"Yes, you got her out in time, but her face is badly burnt and one of her arms, too. You'd better go to hospital yourself. Look at your hands!"

Hamish surveyed his scorched hands. "They are right painful."

"See that he gets treated, Fraser," said Daviot to

Dick. "And, Fraser, you had better type out Macbeth's report for him. His hands will be too sore."

Hamish was glad when his hands were finally attended to. The excitement of Heather's capture had made him forget the pain, but it had just begun to make him feel very sick.

Dick drove him back to the police station. He gave Hamish two of the sleeping pills he had collected from the hospital and helped him into bed. Sonsie and Lugs climbed onto the bed as well and soon all were asleep.

Elspeth called late the following morning. She was furious. "Daviot has refused to give me permission to interview you," she raged. "He, Jimmy, and Blair held a press conference, taking all the credit."

"Well, that's how it should be," said Hamish, gratefully accepting a cup of coffee from Dick with his bandaged hands. "You know how I feel about promotion. Too much attention from the press and they'd feel obliged to move me to Strathbane. Let them have the glory. Sit down, have a cup o' coffee, and I'll give you lots of background."

"So let's get this straight," said Elspeth when he had finished. "How did she get into the country?"

"They found a false passport in a rented car. It was parked up in the High Street in Cnothan."

"So either Sean or Heather murdered Brenda,

Gilchrist murdered Morag and Fergus, and Heather may have come back to Scotland to silence Hannah, but failed and Sean finished her off?"

"Something like that," said Hamish. "Unless she decides to speak, we may never know."

The phone in the office rang. Hamish went to answer it. Elspeth and Dick waited expectantly until he came back.

"Some forensics are just in," said Hamish. "In the wall with the body, they found a broken bottle. She died from a blow to the head, and Heather's fingerprints are on the bottle. And get this. Brenda's body was full of drugs. They may have planned just to keep her sedated until they decided what to do. Now the locals have started talking. A woman says she saw Brenda staggering up the main street on the night Morag was drugged. She looked in the window of the pub, maybe seeing if someone in there could help her. Sean came running after her. He spoke to her and guided her into a car and drove off. I've said it before and I'll say it again: I feel like arresting the whole of that damn village for obstructing the police in their enquiries. Some of the villagers now say they wanted everything to settle down because they were terrified of the factory closing."

"You know what we highlanders are like," said Elspeth. "Very secretive. I'll just go outside the waterfront and make my report. I won't mention you, don't worry. But why cash for the staff? I mean, don't they get paid by cheque?"

"Jimmy says that the new accountant, a Polish woman, spilled the beans. Gilchrist cut the price for various foreign customers, provided they paid cash. Of course, a lot of legitimate business was put through the books. The staff hadn't been paid for a month. I think he was saving up to make a run for it. And Heather knew about it. There was close to a million in cash in the safe."

Heather slowly regained consciousness. Memory came flooding back. She felt no remorse. Brenda, stupid, dull Brenda, had always been the favourite. There had been a frightening moment when Sean came back with half-drugged Brenda and said he had found her looking in the window of the pub. The first thing Harry Gilchrist had asked was whether Morag had been sketching as usual. She might have seen the face at the window. He ordered Sean to go back, slip something in her drink, and snatch the sketchbook.

Then Harry, all sheep-like, said that Morag was blackmailing him, saying he was the father of her baby. He would lose his good name.

Heather had walked up to Morag's lodgings, heavily disguised, and waited outside. She was in luck. No one was around to see her. She backed her Range Rover up to the door. When Morag came out, she came up behind her and strangled her. She ran up the stairs and pinned a postcard to the door. She dumped the body in the boot and then, during the night, she and Gilchrist had rolled the body up in a bale of T-shirts. They then put the bale away from the others, planning to move it and the body when the hunt for Morag was over, if by any chance the postcard saying she had gone away did not work. But some workers had found the bale and had been prepared to load it with the others when they found the body.

All that planning gone for nothing, and because of one local copper.

One of her arms was bandaged, and the good one was padlocked to the bed.

Somehow, I've got to get out of here, she thought.

Every time a nurse or doctor came to examine her, she feigned unconsciousness.

And then she heard a doctor say: "Better remove that handcuff. We're taking her along to the burns unit to see how she's healing up. She should have been coming out of unconsciousness by now."

Then followed an argument with the nurse about how much sedative had been given.

Heather felt the handcuff being removed and the movement as her bed was wheeled out of the room, past the policeman on guard. She heard the policeman say, "I'd better follow you," and, to her relief, the doctor replied, "No need for that. Keep to your post. We'll have her back shortly."

Along corridors they went. Then she felt the hum of a lift and a sensation of being borne upwards.

Out of the lift, through doors, and then silence. A fading voice of the doctor said, "The burns surgeon, Mr. Gillespie, will be along in a minute. I must get a cup of coffee."

Heather cautiously opened one eye, one half of her burnt face being covered in bandages.

She swung her legs over the bed. It was an effort to stand up. But she was fuelled by a mad desire to escape. She tottered to where surgical gowns and masks were hanging. She put on a gown, a mask, and surgical boots.

The corridor outside was empty. She made her way along, looking in the private rooms until she found one with a woman, lying asleep. She went to her locker and removed her coat, scarf, woollen hat, socks, and shoes. Her handbag was there as well. Heather put on the clothes, slung the handbag over her good arm, and wrapped the scarf around her face. She saw a bottle of morphine pills on the bedside table and slipped them into her pocket. She then made her way to the lift, staggering slightly.

Once outside the hospital, she took a set of car keys out of the stolen handbag and went round the car park, clicking the remote control until a car flashed a welcome.

With a sigh of relief, Heather put the keys in the ignition and drove off.

She had no idea where she was going. All she knew was that for the moment, she was free.

Hamish was horrified when he heard the news of Heather's escape. He was summoned to police headquarters to wait for the videotapes from the hospital, as he had a better chance than most of recognising Heather. But there seemed to be miles of red tape to go through before the hospital released the videos.

Hamish and Jimmy eventually sat down and studied them.

"There she goes, coming out of that room," said Hamish bitterly. "You can just see a bit of her bandages between the scarf and the hat." There was a shot of her leaving reception.

"What about the car park?" demanded Hamish.

A man from hospital security said, "We don't have cameras in the car park."

"Find out who's in that room she came out of," shouted Jimmy. "Oh, the hell with it. Come on, Hamish, let's get there now."

The patient turned out to be an elderly woman, a Mrs. Gloag, suffering from cancer. They found out that her handbag was missing as well as her clothes, and that her wallet with her credit cards and car keys had been in it.

Police, already searching for Heather, were given the registration of the car.

"I can't sit here," said Hamish. "I'm getting out there to see if I can find her."

Heather circled around before finally deciding to dump the car. She had to find somewhere to hide out. She walked slowly across the fields at the back of Lochdubh. And then she saw an isolated cottage up on a brae. As she watched, an elderly man with a long grey beard came out and put a bag of rubbish in a bin outside the house.

That will do nicely, she thought. The pain of her burns was creeping back but she didn't want to take any morphine until she had dealt with the old fool.

Pulling the scarf up round her face again, she made her way up to Angus Macdonald's cottage, staggering from side to side because her legs felt weak, and knocked at the door. The seer answered her knock and stood looking thoughtfully at her.

"Could you give me a drink of water? I don't feel very well," said Heather.

"Come ben," said the seer.

He went into the kitchen. Heather saw a pair of scissors lying on a table. She quickly cut the telephone wire. She would put this old boy at his ease and then stab him. What did one more death matter?

Angus came back and handed her a glass of water.

He knew exactly who she was. A quick glance told him his phone had been cut, and his mobile was on the kitchen counter. But he wanted to capture her himself. Hamish Macbeth had jeered at him for too long about being a fake. If he could outwit her and overpower her, he would phone the press before he even phoned the police.

Heather took some morphine pills and quickly swallowed them. The pain was making her feel faint, but she kept firm hold of the scissors.

Angus banked up the fire and then threw on a pile of fir cones from a basket on the hearth. Heather dragged her chair away from the fire as the heat from it made her burns sing with pain.

Angus settled comfortably back in his battered armchair facing her. "Tell me about yourself," he said.

"I'm just a tourist," said Heather. Night had fallen outside.

"You don't look at all well," said Angus.

Hamish was wearily driving along the waterfront to his police station. He cursed and braked suddenly as the small figures of the Currie sisters appeared in his headlights.

"What the hell are you playing at?" he demanded, jumping down from the Land Rover.

"There's a drunk woman gone up to Angus's place," said Nessie.

"Place," echoed her infuriating sister.

"It's your duty to go and see the old man is all right."

Hamish was about to tell them to forget it, but he suddenly asked, "What was she wearing?"

"A blue tweed coat and a woolly hat. Staggering all over the place."

"Out of my way," shouted Hamish, jumping in the Land Rover.

He went on to the police station and called to Dick. "Get ready. We're paying a call on Angus."

"You're not a tourist," Angus was saying. "You're Heather Camford. Are you going to kill me?"

"I just need a place to rest up," said Heather. "Do what you're told and you won't get hurt."

What she really planned to do was wait until the pain abated and stab him in the neck with the scissors.

Angus cursed his own vanity. He should have phoned Hamish from his mobile when he was getting that glass of water for her in the kitchen.

"Why did you kill your own sister?" he asked.

"Because she always had it all. I was engaged to Harry Gilchrist. Then our parents died and precious Brenda got most of the money and Harry dumped me."

"So why on earth did you get into this mess for a man who dumped you?"

"Because he showed me a way to get money and

travel. Brenda would never even leave Scotland. Although she was a year older, we looked pretty much alike, except she was a bore. The crunch came when Harry saw her will. She was going to leave everything to our brother, Luke."

Angus could sense her getting ready to spring.

"What's that?" she cried.

"The wind's getting up," said Angus.

"I swear I heard something."

She rose to her feet and went to the window. Angus jumped up from his chair and grabbed her by her bad arm. She screamed in pain and stabbed him viciously with the scissors just as the door crashed open and Hamish Macbeth hurtled into the room. Dick came hurrying in from the back door, and together they wrestled the screaming woman to the ground.

Hamish clipped on the handcuffs while Dick phoned for help. "Get an ambulance as well," ordered Hamish. "Are you badly hurt, Angus?"

"She got me in the shoulder," said Angus. "I turned a bit away in time or she'd have got me in the heart." Heather had lost consciousness, overcome by the pain in her bad arm.

"Have you got a first-aid kit?" Hamish asked.

"In the top kitchen cupboard on the left."

Hamish went into the kitchen and came back with a box of medical supplies. He swabbed the cut with iodine, put a patch of lint over it, and taped it. "You'll need stitches," he said. "Did she confess to anything?"

"Yes, pretty much. She really hated her sister. Did you know that Gilchrist was going to marry Heather until Brenda inherited the money?"

"No, we didn't know that," said Hamish, silently cursing Daviot from preventing his investigations into Gilchrist.

Police, who had been searching the area, were quickly on the scene. But they had to wait for an ambulance.

When it finally arrived and Heather was being loaded onto a stretcher, that was when they found she had been faking unconsciousness. As the paramedics were carrying her out, she rolled off the stretcher and began to run off down the brae.

Cursing, Hamish ran after her, caught up with her, dived, and brought her down.

He cautioned her and dragged her to her feet while she cursed and spat at him.

When Heather was finally taken away, Hamish turned to Dick. "I would never at any time have supported the idea of the death penalty. But when I look at a creature like that who'll probably end up in some cosy psychiatric unit, I could almost wish we still had it."

Another ambulance, to take Angus to hospital, drove up to the cottage. "I'm going with him," said Hamish.

"I'd better get back to the station," said Dick.

"Hadn't you better come with me?"

"Well," said Dick, "someone's got to look after Sonsie and Lugs."

Hamish hesitated. He should be treating Dick like a policeman and not like an animal keeper.

"Oh, all right," he said. "Just write up a report. I'll do mine later."

Hamish drove to the hospital in Strathbane. He wanted a further talk with Angus and to make sure there was no chance of Heather escaping again. But Blair, Daviot, and Jimmy were waiting for him to get a report. Daviot and Jimmy were pleased but Blair was furious.

When they finally left him to check on Heather, Hamish made his way down to the emergency department where Angus's wound was being stitched.

"Will he be staying in?" Hamish asked the doctor.

"He wants to go home. He seems well enough. He's lost some blood. I think he should rest for an hour or so."

Hamish pulled a chair up to the bed. When the doctor had left, he asked Angus, "What is puzzling me is the time factor. Didn't you recognise her? Her description was on radio and television."

"Aye, I recognised her right away."

"Let me get this straight. I was stopped by the Currie sisters who saw her going up to your cottage. Why didn't you phone?"

"She cut the wires."

"But you've got a mobile, haven't you?"

Angus looked shifty. "I tried," he lied. "But you know how it is. Often it's hard to get a signal."

"Havers." Hamish's hazel eyes sharpened. "You wanted to arrest her yourself and get all the glory."

"I'm a poor auld man," wailed Angus. "I need to rest." He closed his eyes.

"I hope it hurts," said Hamish. He went off to find out how they were getting on with Heather and get his hands treated and rebandaged because the bandages had come loose when he had brought Heather down. Daviot had left but Jimmy and Blair were still there and Blair took great pleasure in ordering Hamish back to his police station.

Outside the hospital, the press had gathered and were being addressed by Daviot. Hamish quietly crept away but then heard Elspeth calling him.

He turned round. "You'll need to stick to the official statement, Elspeth. But I've a wee story for you. Get away from the others and go into emergency. You'll find the seer, Angus Macdonald, there. He'll have a grand story for you. It was his cottage she was caught in. He'll be leaving soon as well, so you'll get some good film of him inside his home. Scenes of Crimes will have gone over the place by now."

"Thanks, Hamish. You're a star."

Hamish climbed into his Land Rover. He drove to Lochdubh under the beautiful, pitiless stars of Sutherland, shining far above the nasty crimes of humans. There was nothing, thought Hamish, like the old, old county of Sutherland with its vast mountains and acres of woodland for making a man feel he was only renting some temporary space on the planet.

When he got to the police station, Dick fussed over him, serving him a dish of venison stew and pouring him a glass of wine. Although Hamish was grateful, not for the first time did he wish Dick would behave more like a policeman and less like a wife.

After he had eaten, he typed up his report. Heather should be secure enough. A policewoman was sitting guard in her hospital room.

Heather recovered consciousness at four in the morning. Slowly, memory came back and with it all the fear and rage of a trapped animal. She twisted her head. A tall policewoman was asleep on a chair beside the bed. Heather raised her good arm. They had not thought it necessary to padlock her with a guard in the room. She tore out the morphine drip and slowly eased herself out of bed, rage giving her superhuman strength. She picked up a bedpan and brought it down on the policewoman's head.

Heather worked quickly, getting the policewoman

out of her uniform. She knew she would have to be fast before the numbing effect of the drugs wore off. The bandages on her face would have to go. Panting, she took them off. She put on the policewoman's clothes and crammed the police hat down on her head.

She put the belt round her, detaching the stun gun and holding it ready.

"Where are you going at this time of night?" demanded Mary, long-suffering wife of Detective Chief Inspector Blair.

"I'm going tae the hospital."

"Why?"

"Shut your face and go back to sleep."

Blair was furious that once more Hamish Macbeth had snatched glory from him. He had been unable to sleep. Then it had occurred to him that if he visited Heather and she had regained consciousness, he might get some more information out of her.

He drove to the hospital and took the lift up to the private rooms on the top floor.

He was just walking along the corridor when he saw a tall policewoman hurrying towards him. "Why aren't you on guard?" he shouted.

Heather raised the stun gun, and shot volts of electricity into the detective's fat chest.

Then she stepped over his body and hurried on her way. A night nurse found Blair ten minutes later. She recognised the detective and assumed he had suffered from a heart attack and summoned help. Blair recovered fifteen minutes later and howled for help.

Hamish was dreaming that he and Priscilla were out in the loch in a small dinghy. There was no wind, and the water was like glass. Priscilla sat beside him at the tiller. "Kiss me, Hamish," she said.

He bent his head to her but someone was shouting and shouting.

Hamish awoke with a start. "Get up, Hamish," said Dick. "You'll never believe this. It's like *The Night of the Living Dead*. The damn bitch has got away again."

Heather hailed a taxi outside the hospital. "Lochdubh," she ordered.

"Havenae you got your police car?" asked the driver.

"Shut up and drive. This is an emergency."

Heather stopped the taxi at the foot of the brae leading up to Angus's cottage. She needed to rest and hide out, and that old fool would be kept in hospital.

She had no money so she curtly told the driver to send the bill to police headquarters.

Clouds were blocking out the starlight. She unhitched a torch from her belt and shone it towards the cottage. Heather drew in a sharp breath of alarm. Police tape fluttered in a rising wind, and a policeman was on guard. Then she remembered she was in uniform.

"Come to relieve me?" said the policeman. "These lazy sods at SOCO won't be here to go over the place until morning."

Heather took out her stun gun, and before the police guard realised what was happening she had shot 650 volts into him. What a handy lot of equipment there was on this belt, thought Heather. She snapped open a collapsible truncheon and brought it viciously down on his head. There were some old sacks lying by the door. She covered his body with them and then went inside the cottage, relieved to find the door unlocked.

Angus felt elated as the television crew drove him home. He loved publicity.

As they were approaching the cottage, Angus suddenly cried, "Stop!"

The soundman who was driving threw on the brakes. "What!"

"I sense something bad," said Angus.

"Very impressive," said the soundman cynically. "Save it for the camera."

He drove on and the van lurched up the brae towards the door of the cottage. "Damn," he said on seeing the police tape. "We'll need to film outside, Elspeth, and then get him to a hotel."

They climbed down from the van. "Sit there while we set up the equipment," said Elspeth.

It just wasn't fair, thought Angus. An outside shot could not compare with one of him in his armchair by the fire. He had carefully arranged his living room to impress customers, from the blackened kettle on its chain over the peat fire to the bits of old farming implements hanging from the beams.

Heather had settled down in Angus's armchair. She had built up the fire. She had found the morphine pills where she had left them and had swallowed a handful with a glass of Angus's precious twelve-year-old malt whisky. Her eyes were just beginning to close when the living room became flooded with a blue-and-white light. She rose and staggered to the window and looked out.

The cameraman, peering through the lens, let out a cry. Heather had removed the police cap and her burned and scarred face looked out like something in a horror film.

Angus got down from the van. "It's her!" he shouted. "Get her! It's Heather Camford!"

Hamish was getting ready for bed when he heard the kitchen door burst open and Archie Maclean's voice cry out, "What's going on up at the seer's cottage, Hamish? There's light and shouts."

Cursing, Hamish pulled his trousers back on and called to Dick to get ready.

Elspeth tried to pull Angus back as he made for his front door. "I'll phone the police. She's dangerous."

But Angus pulled free. He rushed into his living room. Heather stood in front of the red glow of the peat fire, brandishing a small scythe she had taken down from a hook.

"Back!" she snarled, swiping at him with the scythe. Angus saw the truncheon lying on the table and seized it. Behind him, Elspeth was screaming for help. Angus ducked under the scythe and cracked Heather with a great swinging blow across her legs, hearing the bones crack. She staggered back and fell full length. Her head landed right into the glowing peats.

Angus grabbed her legs and pulled her out. Elspeth rushed to the kitchen and came back with a jug of water which she threw over Heather. Hamish came cannoning in the door and stopped short as, with one last horrible eldritch scream of pain, Heather Camford died.

"I didnae mean...," babbled Angus. "Not like this. I wass protecting maself. 'Twas an accident."

"What a shot!" said the white-faced cameraman.

"You filmed it?" exclaimed Hamish.

"Got it all."

"Hand over that film."

"Are you kidding? This is the shot of a lifetime."

"Then I would like to make a statement, Elspeth," said Hamish. "I want to say that while old Angus was being threatened by a murderer, this man, instead of helping, callously filmed the whole thing."

"Oh, you can have the film," said the cameraman sulkily.

"Did you call the police?" asked Hamish.

"Yes, I dialled 999."

"I think I hear sirens," said Hamish. "Let's go outside. The smell of roast Heather is sickening."

Outside, a faint groan alerted them to the policeman under the sacks. While Dick went to help him, police cars and ambulances raced up the brae.

"I wonder how they got here so quickly," said Hamish. "They must have been scouring the area for her. How on earth did she escape again? That uniform she had on must have been taken from the policewoman on guard."

Jimmy came panting up. "Where is she?"

"In there. Very dead. She tried to kill Angus. He fought back and she ended up in the fire."

"Well, that should give her a foretaste of where she's going," said Jimmy.

"Take a statement from Angus first and let him get off to the Tommel Castle Hotel. Elspeth, you can do any interview there. I'll give you a full report of what happened, Jimmy, and then you can get a statement from Angus later."

"I'll try, Hamish," she said weakly. "But I'm feeling very sick."

Down below, lights were going on in all the cottages and dark figures were beginning to emerge.

Hamish drew Jimmy aside. "Put Angus's killing of the damn woman in the best light. You know how it is these days. They're quite capable of charging the auld man wi' murder."

"Don't worry, Hamish. He'll be shown as a desperate, frail old man fighting for his life against a psychotic serial killer. But if you want some good news on this awful night, Blair went to the hospital hoping to have a word with her before anyone else. She had already got the uniform on, and she downed him with a stun gun."

"But what a mess it all is," mourned Hamish. "Elspeth, I'm depending on you to get me that film."

"What film?" demanded Jimmy.

"It's a DVD I want to watch," said Hamish.

"How can you be thinking of your home entertainment at a time like this?" snapped Jimmy. "Elspeth, I won't keep you, but after we finish up here, we'll call on you at the hotel to take statements from you and your crew."

Dawn was lighting the sky when Hamish and Dick eventually made their weary way back to the police station.

Hamish tried to sleep, but, exhausted though he was, he was haunted with visions of Heather's awful death.

He awoke late in the morning to the sound of the telephone ringing and hammering on the door.

"It's the press. Don't answer any of it," said Dick coming in with a cup of coffee. "Man, I still feel sick and I can't seem to get the smell of burning out of my nostrils."

"Where are Sonsie and Lugs?" asked Hamish.

"I took them up to the hotel before I went to bed and got Elspeth to look after them. You don't want the press getting shots of your wild cat."

"You're a good man, Dick," said Hamish, suddenly guilty that he had recently been wishing he could get rid of him. "I don't know what I'd do without you. I'd better get up and get to work. Daviot must be spitting bullets. Heather escaping twice can hardly cover the police in glory. Oh, God, there'll be investigations and reports required. The whole of the next few months is going to be hell."

Once Hamish had finished a long report, he and Dick, noticing that the press had gone, made their way up to the Tommel Castle Hotel. They parked at the side and made their way through the kitchen door, knowing that some of the press were probably trying to get a statement from Angus, while the rest would be over at Strathbane.

Clarry, the chef, was cooking up liver for Sonsie and Lugs, who were standing at his feet, waiting expectantly.

"We'll just nip up the back stairs," said Hamish.

"Had your breakfast?" asked Clarry.

"Haven't had time to eat anything," said Hamish.

"When you come back down, I'll have something for you."

"Do you know which room Elspeth is in?"

"She's got the tower suite, her being a celebrity and all."

Elspeth answered the door to them. "Thank goodness I know how to operate a camera," she said. "Peter, the cameraman, went into shock and had to be sedated. I hope I don't get into trouble with the unions. Got a good interview. Angus is as tough as old boots. I destroyed that film. I don't suppose anyone wants that as a souvenir. If Strathbane saw that, with all the enquiries going on, they might arrest him out of spite."

"Will you be leaving soon?" asked Hamish.

"No. A lawyer's being flown up. We're signing up Angus for an exclusive. I'm bone-weary, Hamish. The police have taken a statement from me, so you don't need to bother."

"I didnae come for that. I came to see you were all right."

"It'll take me a long time. I'm not as hardened as you."

"I'm not that hardened."

"What about that remark about the smell of roasting Heather? Another journalist would have seized on it."

"The worse the situation, the worse the remark. I'll hae bad dreams for a while."

"Angus is the strongest of all of us. He believes in hellfire and in the old Celtic gods. He believes they rode down from the heavens to save him."

"Do you think we might have dinner this evening like old times, Elspeth?"

"All right. If I don't get too tied up here."

"The Italian place at eight?"

"As long as you're not hassled by reporters."

"We should be all right. Apart from yourself, Willie Lamont doesn't like the press. He'll have told them it's all booked up. Anyway, you know what they're like. Come evening, they'll all be in the bar up here, competing to tell the tallest story."

Hamish and Dick enjoyed a gourmet lunch in the kitchen that left them realising they were bone-tired and hadn't had enough sleep. They both went back to the station and to their respective beds. Hamish was sure that Jimmy would not want to contact him. Strathbane would still be coping with answers as to why Heather had escaped a second time.

In the evening, he put on his one good suit and brushed his fiery hair until it shone.

A fine drizzle was falling as he walked along to the restaurant.

Elspeth's hair was once more smooth. She was wearing a grey cashmere sweater and jeans. But her silver Gypsy eyes surveyed him, giving his heart a lurch. No matter how sophisticated she looked, Hamish realised she would always be the Elspeth of the Highlands for him.

"I'm tired," said Elspeth. "It's been a long day. Just a salad for me, Willie."

"Aye, that'll be because of your weight," said Willie. "You television ladies have aye got to starve yourselves."

"I don't put on weight," snapped Elspeth. "I'm just too tired to eat much."

Willie sniggered. "If you say so. But the everdupeas is a sore point for…"

"What the hell's he talking about?" demanded Elspeth.

"He means avoirdupois," said Hamish. "I'll have the lasagne and buzz off, Willie, or I'll put your head in the pizza oven."

"So is Angus all signed up?"

"Signed and sealed. He drives a hard bargain. The other press don't know yet so there won't be any spoiling pieces about him tomorrow, and by that time he'll be a hero. I gather the whole business about the factory is a legal muddle."

"I've been asleep this afternoon," said Hamish, "and I forgot to find out if they arrested people for the fire."

"Not one. The whole village clammed up. Police did a house-to-house search but couldn't find anything. Not even a smell of petrol on anyone."

"Well, all's well that ends so messily," said Hamish. "Back to the quiet life. What about you? Plan to go on forever?"

"I'm a woman. I can't. You won't see any old female presenters. Men can go on getting grey hair and wrinkles, but women are out as soon as they show signs of age. I like the fame and the money, but occasionally I just want to chuck the lot up. It would be nice to leave while I'm at the top."

"How's Barry Dalrymple?"

"Not romancing any of the competition that I know of. Talking of competition...oh, here's our food."

She waited until Willie had left. She lifted a forkful of salad to her mouth and put it down again. "Hamish, did you sleep with Hannah Fleming? She said you did."

Hamish wanted to lie. He found himself going red under her steady gaze. He sighed. "It's like this, Elspeth. She seemed such a beauty. I neffer even listened to the lassie. I'm that ashamed. It was worse when I found everything about her seemed to be false—hair, eyelashes, breasts, teeth, you name it."

"I wonder that didn't put Barry off," said Elspeth. "He swore he hadn't slept with her. He thought she was holding out for marriage."

Hamish poked dismally at his food.

"Don't look sad, Hamish. You were just behaving like any other man."

"I thought I was different," mourned Hamish.

She leaned across and took his hand in a warm clasp. "Let's forget about it. It's over and done with."

He looked into those Gypsy eyes, those silvery eyes, and grasped her hand tightly.

"Marry me, Elspeth."

"What?"

"Why don't we get married?"

"But what about Dick?"

"He'll need to find somewhere else."

"What about my career? Would you move to Glasgow?"

"No, I belong up here and so do you. Why don't we chust get engaged and take it from there?"

"We'd need to keep quiet about it for a bit," said Elspeth, although her eyes were shining. "If I announce I'm getting married, believe me, they'll start looking for a replacement right away."

"Is that a yes?"

"Yes."

Hamish leaned across the table and kissed her full on the mouth. Then he sat back, feeling happy and elated.

"Let's go and tell Dick when we've finished our meal."

Dick was lounging on the sofa with the dog and the cat beside him when Hamish and Elspeth walked in. He took one look at their glowing faces and his heart sank.

"You've got to keep quiet about this, Dick," said Hamish. "Be the first to congratulate us. We're going to get married."

Dick got slowly to his feet. "That's just great. Will I get some drinks?"

"No, I'm taking Elspeth back to the hotel."

"Good luck to both of you."

Hamish and Elspeth went off.

Dick sank slowly back on the sofa and patted the cat's large head. He looked sadly around at what he had come to think of as his little kingdom. His fingers tightened on the cat's fur, and Sonsie gave a warning hiss.

"Over my dead body," said Dick. "Hear that, fellows? Over my dead body."

Epilogue

Thou tyrant, tyrant Jealousy,
Thou tyrant of the mind!

—John Dryden

After two days, Elspeth returned to Glasgow after bidding a passionate farewell to Hamish.

Once she was back in her old environment and back to her usual work, Lochdubh and Hamish seemed very far away. She wondered if she could get him to change his mind and come to live in Glasgow. That would mean the dog and cat as well. Hamish would not leave them behind. And in the smart riverside block of flats in which she lived, pets were forbidden.

She went out one evening with some of her colleagues. They laughed and talked shop and all got mildly drunk. How on earth would Hamish fit in?

On the other hand, she could get out of it all and go back to her old reporting job on the *Highland Times*.

But her mind cringed away from the thought of reporting things like school concerts, flower shows, and council meetings.

At the Tommel Castle Hotel, the manager, Mr. Johnson, felt uneasy. His loyalty was to the hotel and that meant to Priscilla. Like all good hotel managers, he knew who was sleeping with whom, and Hamish had spent two nights with Elspeth Grant. She had not been wearing an engagement ring, but when she had leaned forward to put her debit card in the machine in the manager's office, her neckline had dipped and Mr. Johnston had clearly seen what looked like a diamond engagement ring worn on a thin chain around her neck.

A week after Elspeth had left, he was down at Patel's grocery shop to buy the thin cigars that Mr. Patel kept for him when he saw Dick Fraser entering the shop.

He paid for his cigars and waylaid Dick.

"Come outside. I want a word with you."

Somehow, Mr. Johnson knew that if he asked if Hamish and Elspeth were engaged, then Dick might deny it outright, so instead he said, "What's all this about Hamish going to marry Elspeth Grant?"

Taken aback, Dick said, "How did you hear about it?"

"Little bird told me."

"Keep quiet about it!"

"Sure. But I wonder what our Priscilla would think about it? Don't worry. I won't breathe a word."

Priscilla, thought Dick, forgetting about shopping and staring for a long time over the loch. Now, there was a thing. Priscilla would be a beautiful spanner to throw in the works.

He had arranged with Hamish that when the couple were married, he would put a caravan up on the back field and move there. He felt that the police station was now more his than Hamish's. Hadn't he cleaned and polished and furnished until it was his little palace?

He was sure that deep down in Hamish, there was a part that had never got over Priscilla. He did not know what had gone wrong to end their engagement.

What would Priscilla do if she found out?

He got into his battered car, drove to the hotel, and walked into the manager's office.

"I've been thinking about Priscilla," said Dick, settling into a chair on the other side of the manager's desk. "Maybe you feel she ought to be told, but that might be a bad idea. I was a wee bit worried that your loyalty to the Halburton-Smythe family might make you want to tell her."

"I really don't think Hamish means anything to her any more," said Mr. Johnson.

"Oh, that's all right, then," said Dick blithely. "And here's me worried that the lassie would mind."

"She hardly comes up here any more," said Mr. Johnson, half to himself. "Probably wouldn't bother her at all. What would bother her is the news was being kept from her."

Dick folded his chubby hands over his stomach and smiled. "Just what I was beginning to think."

"Coffee?"

"No, I'd better get back. Not a word to Hamish. Mind!"

Hamish opened his newspaper. The death of Heather and the subsequent investigations had gone from the front page. But on one of the inside pages was a photograph of Freda Crichton, along with photographs of models wearing her creations and the news that she had secured a job with the Jacques Desonet fashion house in Paris.

He found Freda's number and phoned her to congratulate her, saying that he had been worried all her designs had gone up in smoke.

"The best ones were down in Inverness for the fashion show," said Freda. "And I had kept my best sketches at home. I've got that publicist, Joan Friend, to thank for all this."

Hamish wished her luck and rang off, glad that some good news had come out of the disaster.

*   *   *

Mr. Johnson phoned Priscilla. "Just to bring you up to date with the news," he said. "Hamish Macbeth is getting married."

Priscilla laughed. "If he gets to the altar this time, it'll be a miracle. First it was that immigrant he thought he was saving from deportation, then it was that conniving drunk. Elspeth saved him from the last one."

"Well, it seems like the real thing this time around. Priscilla! Are you still there?"

"Yes, who is he marrying."

"Elspeth Grant."

"Oh." Another long silence. Then, "Thank you for telling me," and Priscilla rang off.

Elspeth was due to arrive at the weekend. On the Saturday morning, Dick went out for a walk with Sonsie and Lugs as Hamish pottered about, putting clean sheets on his bed and flowers on the kitchen table.

Hamish heard a car drive up and stop outside the station. He flung open the door, a glad smile of welcome on his face.

The smile faded as Priscilla walked towards him, carrying a large box.

Feeling irrationally guilty, Hamish said, "Grand to see you. What's in the box?"

"It's an engagement present for you," said Priscilla.

"How did you know I was engaged?"

"Mr. Johnson told me."

"It's supposed to be a secret," said Hamish angrily. "How the hell did he know?"

"It leaks like a sieve up here," said Priscilla. "Aren't you going to ask me in?"

"Of course." Hamish took the box from her and stood aside to let her past.

Priscilla put the box on the kitchen table. She was wearing a pale blue sweater, as blue as her eyes. Her golden hair shone in the sunlight streaming through the kitchen window.

"Aren't you going to open it?" she asked.

Hamish got a knife and slit the Scotch tape sealing the box. He unwrapped one tissue-wrapped object. It was a beautiful cut-crystal whisky glass.

"There are six of them," said Priscilla. "You don't need to unwrap them all now."

The phone in the office rang. Hamish went to answer it.

Elspeth's voice came on the line. "There's a terrible massacre in Libya," she said. "I have to be here to do all the reports coming in. I'm so sorry. I'll be up next weekend." A voice in the background could be heard calling her. "Got to go. Sorry."

Hamish slowly put down the receiver.

Then he dialled the Tommel Castle Hotel. When he got the manager, he asked, "Do you know how Priscilla got to hear of my engagement?"

"It was me. She was on the phone and I happened to mention it."

"And who told you?"

"Nobody. I noticed Elspeth was wearing an engagement ring around her neck and put two and two together."

"Did Dick tell you?"

"Absolutely not."

"When I'm investigating a crime," complained Hamish, "no one up here seems to have seen or heard anything, but when it comes to my private business, I may as well put a neon sign on the hotel roof. Have you told anyone else?"

"Not a soul."

"Well, don't!" Hamish slammed down the phone and returned to the kitchen.

"I heard all that," said Priscilla. "Why such a secret?"

"Elspeth's frightened that if her boss hears about it, he'll start looking for a replacement."

"If she's keeping her job, how will that work out?"

"Probably commute at the weekends until we figure something out. Sit down. Want coffee?"

"Yes, please."

"Dick's got some ready."

"What about Dick? What happens to him?"

"He's going to get a caravan and put it up on the field at the back."

"Poor Dick. It'll be like getting a divorce."

"Cut that out, Priscilla. I'm not married to the man. Here's your coffee and some shortbread.

"I havenae thanked you for the present," Hamish continued gruffly. "Verra kind of you."

Realising from the strength of Hamish's highland accent that he was thoroughly upset, Priscilla said gently, "Would you like me to leave?"

"Yes…no. As a matter of fact, I booked a table for lunch. Care to join me?"

"That would be nice."

Angus, the seer, had done several television interviews at the studios in Glasgow and had now been run north with a crew for a final take of him standing on the waterfront at Lochdubh, looking nobly out over the loch and pontificating on all the times his amazing insight had helped the police.

As Priscilla and Hamish were walking towards the restaurant, they stopped to watch and listen.

"Would you chust look at the auld fool," said Hamish. "He's wearing white robes."

"Looks quite biblical," said Priscilla and Hamish laughed.

In the restaurant, Willie fussed over Priscilla, and cleaned the table with so much detergent that Hamish got a sneezing fit.

"Some things never change," said Priscilla. "Tell me all about the murders."

Hamish began to speak. He had forgotten what a good listener she was.

Dick, strolling past with the dog and cat at his heels, saw them through the restaurant window. "Please God," he muttered, "let him fall in love with her again."

When he got back to the police station, he was just in time to take a call from Elspeth. "Is Hamish there, Dick? I rather had to cut him off the last time."

"He's gone to the restaurant for lunch."

"Alone?"

"No, Miss Halburton-Smythe is with him."

"I'll phone him there. Goodbye."

Elspeth felt a sharp stab of jealousy. She remembered all the times when it looked as if she and Hamish had been about to get together at last and then Priscilla had appeared on the scene and he had promptly forgotten about her. Then as she looked at the television monitor, she saw film of Angus's waterfront interview, and, as she watched, there was a clear shot of Hamish and Priscilla, standing and watching. Priscilla said something, Hamish laughed, and they walked on.

She dug her fingernails into the palms of her hands. How dare he look so happy and carefree? She was about to phone until she was reminded she was about to present another bulletin.

*   *   *

Hamish found it therapeutic to talk about all the murders with Priscilla, ending up with the horrible death of Heather.

"We're closing up," said Willie.

"Pity," said Hamish. "I havenae talked so much in ages."

"We needn't stop," said Priscilla. "Let's go up to the hotel. We'll take my car. I'm leaving in the morning. This is just a flying visit so let's make the most of it."

The phone in the restaurant rang just after they had left. Willie tried to sound like an answering service. "The restaurant is now closed," he said, "but if you'd like to leave…"

"Willie, it's me, Elspeth. Is Hamish still there?"

"No, he and Miss Halburton-Smythe have just left. My, they were talking so long I had to throw them out. I heard Miss Halburton-Smythe inviting him up to the hotel. You'll get him there."

The highlander that was Elspeth thirsted for revenge. How could Hamish forget about her so easily? She was damned if she would go on chasing him on the phone.

It was a long bitter day, and at the end of it as she was taking off her television make-up, a young researcher, Patty Klein, put her head round the door.

"We're all off to the pub with the Sheratons. Coming?"

"Be right there," said Elspeth.

The Sheratons were like the Chippendales, a group of hunky young men who did a striptease performance for audiences of screaming women. They had been interviewed earlier in the evening.

When Elspeth entered the pub, she got a noisy welcome. All of a sudden, she just wanted to drink and drink and forget Hamish Macbeth.

Hamish had dinner with Priscilla that evening. Afterwards, she ran him back to the police station.

He found Heather's brother, Luke, waiting for him. "I'm trying to find out how my poor sister really died," he said when he saw Hamish.

"It appears Brenda was struck a blow on the head," said Hamish soothingly, "and…"

"I'm not talking about Brenda, I'm talking about Heather."

"Heather received bad burns when she tried to commit suicide by running into the flames of the burning factory," said Hamish. "On her last escape from hospital, she went to Angus Macdonald's cottage where she used a stun gun on a policeman on guard before hitting him. She then stabbed Angus. He shoved her to protect himself and she fell in the fire. That was when she died."

"I don't believe this. I think she died as a result of police brutality."

I wonder if there's madness in this family, thought Hamish wearily.

"Look," he said, "take the matter up with headquarters in Strathbane."

"I have already done so. They gave me the same load of rubbish you have just done. I had hoped for honesty from you."

"And you got it," said Hamish coldly. "Your sister was a stone-hard serial killer."

"You will all be hearing from my lawyers!"

"Do that."

"You haven't heard the last of this."

He stormed off.

Hamish shrugged and went into the office to phone Elspeth. She didn't answer her home phone and her mobile was switched off.

Elspeth awoke the next morning. Her head was hammering and her mouth was dry. Bits of the previous evening came back to her in flashes of memory. She remembered flirting with the leader of the Sheratons, Steve Bunty.

Elspeth looked up at the ceiling and stiffened in horror. She was looking up at a reflection of herself and beside her on the bed was a naked man, lying on his back. It was Steve Bunty.

She swung her legs over the edge of the bed. She was fully dressed. I must have passed out, she thought in a panic. I'd better get out of here before he wakes up. Thank goodness Hamish is up in the Highlands. If he ever got to hear of this, we'd be finished. She glanced at her watch. It was noon. Barry Dalrymple must be looking for her.

Hamish strolled along to Patel's late the following afternoon to buy a copy of the *Scottish Evening Bulletin*. He liked settling down with the crossword, which was easy and made him feel clever.

"Haven't got a copy left," said Mr. Patel.

"How's that? Good story?"

"Mr. Fraser bought every copy in the shop."

Hamish laughed. "Must be some sort of competition in it, although why he wants the whole lot, I can't even begin to imagine."

He could not find Dick in the police station but smoke was drifting from a bonfire up at the back.

If that's Dick, what on earth is he doing? wondered Hamish. He'll choke my sheep with all that smoke.

He ran up to the field at the back. Dick was stuffing piles of newspaper into a fire in an old oil drum.

His back was to Hamish and he did not hear him coming. Hamish seized a newspaper from a pile on the grass. There on the front page was a large headline: ELSPETH GRANT GETS CARRIED AWAY.

Below it was a large photograph of Elspeth flung over the shoulder of a naked man who was wearing nothing but a leather thong. Dick turned round and saw Hamish and hung his head. He had been feeling guilty at trying to break up Hamish's engagement and had been trying to make amends by hiding the news item from him.

Elspeth suffered a lot of teasing at the television studios. What was a drunken horror to her seemed to be a great lark to the rest of them. They had all got very drunk and Steve had performed an impromptu striptease. He had then grabbed Elspeth who hardly knew what was happening and had run off with her. With a large number of the public now having phones that took photographs, they had been snapped outside just as Steve was getting them both into a taxi.

Elspeth looked dismally at her mobile phone. Hamish again. What on earth was she going to say to him?

At last, she finally answered and said in a small voice, "I suppose you've seen the newspaper. I didn't do anything. I just passed out."

"I don't think that really makes it all right," said Hamish slowly. "Your life down there seems foreign tae me. I don't think I really know you, Elspeth."

"What about you, Mr. High and Mighty?" demanded Elspeth. "Yes, I went out to get drunk because every time I phoned Lochdubh all I heard was that you were wining and dining Priscilla."

"That's different. She's an old friend."

"Like hell she is!"

"So it's my fault you're smooching a stripper?"

"Exactly."

"You're mad."

"I suppose you want your ring back?"

"Keep it. It'll remind you of dear Steve."

Elspeth rang off. Hamish sat for a long time with his head in his hands. Then he went into the living room where Dick was sitting sadly looking at a catalogue of caravans.

"You can put that catalogue away, Dick," said Hamish quietly. "The engagement's off."

"Och, Hamish, I'm right sorry. Is there anything I can do?"

"No, find something on that TV of yours. I don't want to think."

Dick scrolled through the selections on the menu and settled on an American cop show.

Hamish stared at it blindly for ten minutes and then said abruptly, "I'm off for a walk."

He met Angela Brodie on the waterfront. "I saw the evening paper," she said.

"So Dick didn't manage to buy up all of them?"

"I'm afraid not. Unfortunately, the Currie sisters

got hold of one first. It's all over the village. Poor Elspeth."

"Why poor Elspeth?"

"It must be awful being a celebrity."

They leaned on the waterfront in silence. Angela looked sideways at Hamish's downcast face.

"I think that news item really upset you, Hamish."

"It did. The fact is, we were engaged to be married and now it's all off."

"Oh, Hamish, did she explain?"

"She heard I'd been dining with Priscilla and went out to get drunk."

"I can understand that, Hamish. Everyone knows you've always had a yen for Priscilla."

"Yes, but I know nothing of Elspeth's lifestyle down there. Her friends would probably think I was some sort of hick from the sticks. She'd only be able to see me at weekends. What happens if we have a row? She'd probably end up in another scandal."

"That's a bit hard."

"I'd neffer be able to trust her again."

And she won't be able to trust you, thought Angela sadly.

"What about the Palfours?" she asked.

"The case comes up in a month. I'll have to go to the High Court to testify."

"Have they arrested anyone else who worked at the factory?"

"No, why?"

"There was something about a lot of money in the safe. Why wasn't it in the bank?"

Hamish told her.

"But surely the accountant was in on it. Or Gilchrist's secretary."

"He evidently persuaded his Polish accountant that he liked to keep a certain amount of cash out of the bank because he didn't trust banks. He said he would eventually declare it and pay taxes on it. She desperately needed the work and so she went along with it."

"I suppose no one trusts banks these days. That lot from the bank who were wining and dining at the hotel were ordering the most expensive wines, despite the fact that the bank had to be bailed out with taxpayers' money. Oh, here's the minister. I think he's looking for you. See you soon."

Angela walked off as the minister, Mr. Wellington, came up to join Hamish. "I just wondered if you were in need of some spiritual help," he said.

"No, no, I'm chust fine," said Hamish, embarrassed.

"I always find forgiveness is the thing," said Mr. Wellington solemnly. "God will help you forget the horrors of murder."

"Aye, well, I'll remember that," said Hamish, shuffling his boots. "Got to go. Got a report to write."

"Remember! Forgiveness!" called the minister after him.

Odd wee man, thought Hamish. But living with that bully of a wife is enough to make anyone strange.

When Hamish returned to the police station, Dick said, "Sit yourself down and I'll get your supper."

Hamish looked around the cosy kitchen. Time to count my blessings, he thought. The murders are solved, life is quiet again, and I've still got my police station.

And somewhere out there, there's some girl who would make a grand wife. All I have to do is wait… and hope.

SAVOR THE FLAVORS
OF SCOTLAND—
WITH ANOTHER
HAMISH MACBETH MYSTERY
BY **M. C. BEATON**!

*Please turn the page
for a preview of*

Death *of a* Policeman

A watched pot never boils.

—Mid-nineteenth-century proverb

The fact that all the police forces in Scotland were to be amalgamated into one large force struck terror into police headquarters in Strathbane. It was said that all over Scotland three thousand auxiliary jobs would be lost, which would mean more work for the actual police themselves. Then they would start chopping heads of the very police force itself.

Only one man was happy about the news—Detective Chief Inspector Blair. Surely this might be the opportunity to get rid of Police Sergeant Hamish Macbeth and winkle him out of his cosy station in Lochdubh. He could not understand how Hamish had been able to hang on with local police stations closing down all over Scotland.

But he experienced a setback when he broached the

idea to his chief, Superintendent Daviot. "Sutherland is a huge county," said Daviot, "and it is surely economical to have Macbeth cover all of it."

"But most of the time, he and his sidekick, Fraser, just mooch around doing nothing," complained Blair.

"We have no proof of that," said Daviot severely. "You should be worried about your own job."

"Whit!"

"I am sure we will have officials soon crawling all over us to see what they can cut," said Daviot.

Blair took himself off to the pub to crouch over a double whisky and try to work out a plan. If he could prove that Hamish Macbeth did little, then he could send a report in to the new authorities. But who would be low enough to spy on Macbeth?

After another double whisky, his brain seemed to clear. Cyril Sessions was a fairly new constable, nick-named Romeo because of his good looks. Shortly after his arrival from Perth, Blair had uncovered evidence that Cyril had been enjoying the favours of a prostitute, without paying her a penny. She had finally cracked and reported Cyril. Blair got the complaint and confronted Cyril. Cyril had pleaded and begged and said he would do anything if Blair made the complaint go away.

Cunningly, Blair decided to keep this ally in the bank, so to speak, until such time as he would need to draw on him. He phoned headquarters and asked Cyril to join him.

Women in the pub stared appreciatively at Cyril when he entered. He was of medium height with glossy black hair, blue eyes in a square handsome face, and a muscular figure.

"Sit down, my lad," said Blair. "I've a wee job for you. I want evidence that Hamish Macbeth in Lochdubh does bugger all when it comes to policing."

"Isn't that the man who's got a grand reputation for solving murders?"

"I was me that solved them," said Blair, "while that slimy toad took the credit. You owe me a favour, or do I need to remind you that I had to threaten that brass nail to keep her painted mouth shut?"

"Brass nail?"

"Where have you been? Brass nail. Screw. Get it? That prossy you were banging."

"Oh, aye. That."

"Aye, that. Here's what you've got tae do. Take a fishing holiday in Lochdubh and get photos of Macbeth lounging around. His policeman, Dick Fraser, often sleeps in a deck chair in the front garden. Get a good shot o' that. Macbeth doesn't know you, so you can get real close. Chat with the locals. Pick up gossip."

"I don't fish."

"Well, rambling or something like that. The highlands are fu' o' hairy-legged bastards farting ower the hills."

"When do I start?"

"Next week'll do. I want this done and dusted before numpties from the new police arrangement descend on us."

Cyril looked at him shrewdly. "Have you tried this before?"

Blair shifted his fat haunches on the barstool. He had, in fact, and it had ended with his spy nearly getting killed. But he had no intention of telling Cyril anything about it.

"No, just thought o' it," he said. "Get moving and fix that holiday."

Hamish was actually working at that moment. Lairg sheep sales are the biggest in Europe and he was policing them with Dick at his side. Because of the size of the sales, Strathbane had sent up two policemen to assist him. The importance of the yearly event meant that crofters were often dressed in the sort of finery people thought were the reserve of tourists: deer stalkers, tall crooks, kilts and sporrans.

Hamish and Dick strolled into the beer tent late in the day and found their other two colleagues. "Everyone upset about the new Scottish police force?" asked Hamish, joining them.

"You can say that again," said one of them. "Take off the civilian staff, and think o' the extra paperwork."

"And how's my dear friend Blair?" asked Hamish.

The other policeman sniggered, "I think he's in lurv."

"Who's the lucky lady?"

"It's a bloke. Fairly new copper called Cyril Sessions. Real handsome chap. Blair's been seen drinking with him all over the place. Can't get enough of his company."

As they walked out of the beer tent, Dick said sententiously, "It does happen, you know."

"What does?" asked Hamish.

"Fellows when they get on a bit. They wake up to the fact that they prefer other blokes to their missus."

"Oh, aye? Well, the only love affair Blair's ever had is with the booze. He's plotting something."

"Do you mind if I hurry off?" said Dick anxiously. "I'm due down in Strathbane."

"Another quiz?"

"Aye, and the prize is a brand new Volvo."

"Off you go. Things are quiet here."

Hamish switched on the television that evening. Dick had such a reputation for winning quiz competitions that he was surprised they let him on.

The questions seemed to be very difficult. Six contestants were quickly whittled down to two, Dick and a shabby old man. And then Dick lost at the last question: how long does it take light from the moon to reach the earth?

The old man said quickly, "One-point-twenty-six seconds." There was a roll of drums and cheers from the audience as he was led to the gleaming new car.

Hamish waited up until a weary Dick arrived home. "Not like you to lose," said Hamish. "That must be the first time."

"I couldnae do it to him," said Dick.

"What?"

"He was an auld crofter. He'd never been on one of thae quiz shows before. The stories o' hardship he told me in the green room. It would ha' been wicked not to let the poor auld soul win."

"What was his name again?"

"Henry McQueen. Got a bittie o' a place outside Bonar Bridge."

"I wonder if there's anything on the computer about him," said Hamish.

"Why?"

"Just a hunch. I've got a feeling I saw him at the sheep sales."

Dick followed Hamish into the police office. Hamish switched on the computer and searched for Henry McQueen's name. "There's something here from last year's Highland Times," said Hamish, clicking it open. "There you are. I thought I'd heard of him. He took top price for his lambs two years running. You were conned. Oh, here's another link. Five years ago he came out top on Mastermind. Subject, the Epistles of St. Paul."

"I'll murder the auld creep," raged Dick.

"Oh, leave it. I'm sure he'll crop up again," said Hamish soothingly, "and then you can wipe the floor with him."

The following day, Cyril checked into Mrs. Mackenzie's bed and breakfast on the waterfront at Lochdubh. He dumped his haversack in a small room and wondered how long he could put up with pretending to be a rambler, particularly as he had arrived in his car. He had pointed out to Blair that he was surely not going to be able to follow Macbeth around on foot.

The room was at the back of the house. It was cold. There was a meter on the wall with a sign saying that pound coins had to be deposited for electricity. The bed was narrow and covered in rough blankets under a pink candlewick spread. A print of Jesus feeding the multitude with loaves and fishes hung over the blocked-up fireplace. Underneath was the legend "His Eye Is on the Sparrow." On a rickety table by the bed was a large Bible. The room was fairly dark. Cyril popped a coin in the meter and switched on the light in a glass bowl above his head full of dead flies. He hung his clothes in the curtained alcove that served as a wardrobe. There was neither a phone nor a television set. The only reason, he thought, that she got any customers was because Mrs. Mackenzie charged cheap rates.

He decided to go out for a walk around the village and start work.

The day outside was warmer than his room. A pale October sun shone down on a row of whitewashed cottages fronting the sea loch. It looked like a picture postcard. Cyril walked towards the harbour. He brightened when he saw a pub. He would start with a drink and see what he could find out from the locals. There was a silence when he entered. He ordered a vodka and tonic.

A small man in tight clothes materialised at his elbow and said, "Are you on holiday?"

"Yes," said Cyril. "I'm Jamie Mackay up from Perth."

"Archie Maclean," said the little man.

"Let me buy you a drink," said Cyril, "and maybe we could sit over at that table by the window. I'd like to get to know a bit about the village."

Archie ordered a double whisky. Cyril realised that Blair had said nothing about paying for his work. Conversation rose again as they made their way to the table.

"So what are you doing here?" asked Archie.

"I came up by car, but I might do a bit of walking."

Archie's sharp blue eyes in his nut-brown face

dropped to look at Cyril's highly polished black shoes. "I hope you've got boots with you," he said. "You won't get far in those."

"Yes, I've got boots," said Cyril. He wondered why the little man wore such tight clothes, not knowing that Archie's wife washed all his clothes so that they shrank.

"So, much crime around here?" asked Cyril.

"No, it's fair quiet."

"I saw a police station. Not much for a copper to do up here."

"Hamish Macbeth, the police sergeant, covers a big part o' Sutherland," said Archie. "He's got a lot tae do. Thanks for the drink, laddie. Got tae go."

Hamish was seated at the kitchen table when Archie burst through the door. "What's up?" asked Hamish.

"'Member the time when that scunner Blair put a copper on yer tail to report on ye?"

"As if it were yesterday," said Hamish. "Has he sent another?"

"Could be," said Archie, sitting down at the table. "Could I hae wan o' your espresso coffees? The wifie doesnae hold wi' coffee."

"That's Dick's machine. I don't know how to operate it. I'll fetch him. He's sleeping in the garden."

Hamish strolled round to the front of the police station just in time to see the tall figure of Cyril snapping a photograph of Dick asleep in his deck chair. He nipped round onto the road and confronted Cyril. "What's so special about a photograph of a man in a deck chair?" asked Hamish.

"I'm a bit of an amateur photographer," said Cyril. "I thought I'd enter it for a competition and call it 'Sleeping Policeman.'"

"Visiting?"

"Yes. Good place for walks."

"Where are you staying?" asked Hamish.

"Mrs. Mackenzie's. I'll be getting along."

Cyril strode off. Hamish stared after him. Then he went into the office and phoned detective Jimmy Anderson.

"How are things up in peasantville?" asked Jimmy.

"Weird."

"It's aye weird up there."

"There's this fellow turned up and took a photo of Dick asleep in the garden. Handsome chap with curly black hair, tall, blue eyes, little half-moon scar above the right eye, but with policeman's shoes on and black socks. Says he's going to be going for walks. Anyone missing from headquarters that looks like that?"

"There's one smarmy bastard who sucks up to Blair. Cyril Sessions."

"I knew it!" exclaimed Hamish. "Blair is out to get proof that there's no crime up here. I'll get that photo back somehow."

Hamish woke Dick up and explained the situation. He ended by saying, "Let's see if we can lose the cheil for an hour. Give Archie a mug o' espresso first."

They walked over to the harbour fifteen minutes later, where Archie Macleod was sitting on a bollard, rolling a cigarette. "No tourists today?" asked Hamish. Fishing stocks were dwindling, and so Archie supplemented his income by taking tourists on trips round the loch.

"I've only got a couple. They'll be along in a minute."

"Do me a favour. Yon chap you met in the pub is one o' Blair's snoops. He'll be hanging around. He's staying at Mrs. Mackenzie's. Offer him a free trip in your boat."

"Aye, right. Want me to tip him ower the side?"

"No, just keep him away. If he's got his camera with him, try to stage an accident to the camera that makes it look as if it's his fault."

Archie scurried off. He found Cyril outside Mrs. Mackenzie's. Cyril was delighted to accept. It would be a chance to find out more about Macbeth.

Hamish stood at his living room window, watching, until he saw the fishing boat sail out into the loch. Then he hurried along to Mrs. Mackenzie's bed and breakfast.

Before he got there, he met the Currie sisters, twins

Nessie and Jessie, on the waterfront. They were very much alike. Although the day was sunny, there was a nip in the air, and so they had reverted to their winter wear of camel-hair coats, headscarves, and brogues.

"Grand day," said Hamish. "Have you seen the newcomer?"

"We have that," said Nessie. "Like a fillum star."

"Fillum star," echoed the Greek chorus that was Jessie.

"It's refreshing to find a young man who kens so much about the Bible," said Hamish. "He's out with Archie, but when he gets back, you should invite him to tea. Right religious, he is."

"We'll do that," said Nessie. "It will be nice to talk to a clean young man instead o' a lazy philanderer like yourself."

"Like yourself," came her sister's echo.

Hamish walked on and knocked at the door of the bed and breakfast. Mrs. Mackenzie was a small woman wearing a flower-patterned overall with her hair tied up in a headscarf. The lines on her face were permanently set in disapproval.

"Whit?" she demanded.

"I would like a look at the newcomer's room," said Hamish. "We've had a tip-off."

"Then he can pack his bags and get out."

"No, no," said Hamish soothingly. "Don't tell him I called. Chust a routine enquiry. You don't want to go losing a paying customer at this time of year. Chust a wee peek in his room."

"Oh, all right. Top o' the stairs on the left. The door isnae locked. I was up there cleaning."

Hamish nipped up the stairs and into Cyril's room. There was a computer lying on the bed, but what he wanted was the camera. There was no sign of it. He could only hope that Archie would find a way to get rid of it.

Archie let his mate, Ally Harris, take the wheel while he pointed out various landmarks to the two tourists, a husband and wife, and Cyril. Cyril was standing at the side of the boat, his camera slung round his neck.

Moving behind him, Archie took out a sharp knife and sliced almost through the strap at the back of Cyril's neck.

He said, "If youse will look ower the side, that's where the kelpie is supposed tae live."

"What's a kelpie?" asked the female.

"It's a creature that appears as a sea horse and sometimes changes into a beautiful wumman," said Archie. "It goes after wee bairns. It gets them to stroke it and it's adhesive and when they stick to it, it drags them down into the loch and eats them. It's supposed to live right down there. Lean right ower and you'll maybe see it."

Cyril and the tourists leaned over. "There is something down there," said Cyril excitedly. A black shape could be seen moving in the murky depths. His camera was swinging from his neck by the strap. Just as he was reaching for it, the strap broke and his camera dropped down into the water.

A seal surfaced and stared up at them as Cyril let out a wail of dismay.

"You should ha' got yourself wan o' thae wee yins you can carry in your pocket," said Archie. "I hivnae seen wan like that in years. If you go to Patel's shop, you can buy wan o' thae cheap throwaway ones."

"It was a friend's camera," said Cyril. He cursed Blair, who had given him an old Rolleiflex camera out of storage at headquarters, saying it was better than any newfangled one. He did have a Canon pocket one inside his jacket. At least he would be more comfortable using that.

Archie telephoned Hamish to say that Cyril's camera was now somewhere at the bottom of the loch, and Hamish heaved a sigh of relief.

Before, when he had been under threat, he had manufactured a crime wave with the help of the locals. But Hamish was feeling lazy, enjoying the rare good weather of the autumn.

Cyril had read up on Hamish's successful cases and knew that several had taken place in the town of Braikie.

The following day, he decided to visit the town, hoping the residents there might have less favourable ideas about Hamish than the villagers had. He had gone to the village stores and after leaning on the counter, talking about the weather, he had asked the owner, Mr. Patel, what he thought of the local policeman. Mr. Patel had smiled and launched on a paean of praise about Hamish.

Cyril had then gone to the Italian restaurant for dinner and quizzed the waiter, Willie Lamont. His heart sank when it turned out that Hamish was godfather to Willie's child. Was no one going to criticise the man?

But in Braikie, his hopes sank lower. The people he talked to did not know Hamish personally but knew his reputation for solving murders and seemed to be proud to have such a policeman looking after them.

He was passing the library when he noticed a sign outside saying there were books for sale. Cyril decided to buy some light reading and walked into the Victorian gloom of the building.

Hetty Dunstable, the librarian, saw a handsome man looking around and teetered forward on her high heels. "Can I help you?"

Cyril saw a small, thin woman in her early forties wearing a nearly transparent white blouse over a tight skirt. She had a small, pinched face and bulging brown eyes. Cyril thought sourly that she looked like a rabbit with myxomatosis. But he gave his most charming smile and said, "I saw that you had books for sale."

"Yes, they're over here," said Hetty, leading the way to a wooden bench. "These are the ones that are too damaged to remain on the shelves. Are you new to the area?"

"Just on holiday," said Cyril. "I'm over in Lochdubh."

"Keep clear of the police station. Hamish Macbeth is useless."

"I'd like to hear more," said Cyril. "I enjoy a bit of gossip with a pretty girl. When do you get off?"

"We close up in ten minutes."

"Let's go for a drink."

"Yes, I would love that," said Hetty.

Hetty had no intention of telling this gorgeous man her real reason for disliking Hamish. She had once invited Hamish to a party at her flat after having met him on one of his investigations. Hamish was not interested. But she had drunk too much and had thrown herself at him, calling him her darling. Hamish had gently pushed her away and gone home. Her friends teased her about it until she began to think Hamish had wronged her. She told them so many times that Hamish had led her on that she began to believe it.

Cyril was often seen in Hetty's company in the following days. Then, to Hetty's dismay, he said he would be too busy to see her. Hetty began to feel guilty. She was sure Cyril was spying on Hamish and wondered if he was a villain. She had made up a lot of malicious stories about Hamish's laziness. If anything happened to Hamish, the investigation would lead back to her.

She at last phoned Hamish and said someone called Jamie Mackay had been asking a lot of questions about him.

"Don't worry," said Hamish. "I know all about him," correctly guessing that Jamie was Cyril.

"What will you do?" asked Hetty.

"Take my shotgun and blow the bugger's head off," said Hamish and rang off.

"Let's give Cyril something to do tomorrow," Hamish said to Dick. "We'll race off tomorrow up north and give the lad something to chase. The beasties are getting fat. They need some exercise."

Hamish's "beasties" consisted of a wild cat called Sonsie and a dog called Lugs. "I'll get a picnic ready," said Dick.

Hamish felt a stab of irritation. He wished Dick would not be so—well—*domesticated*. He felt Dick was taking the place of a possible wife, and Hamish often dreamed of marriage. His love affair with television presenter Elspeth Grant had recently fallen through. He had once been engaged to Priscilla Halburton-Smythe, daughter of the retired colonel who owned the Tommel Castle Hotel. But Priscilla's sexual coldness had caused him to break off the engagement.

At that moment, Cyril was ensconced in the Currie sisters' parlour, balancing a cup of tea on one knee. He had hoped the sisters would give him some gossip about Hamish, but they seemed hell-bent on quizzing him about the King James Version of the Bible.

"Beautiful words," said Nessie. "'I am the voice of one crying in the wilderness.'"

"I couldn't agree more," said Cyril, ignoring Jessie's echo. He thought, *if I don't get out of this damn place soon I'll go mad.* "You were saying something about the local policeman."

"No, I wasn't," said Nessie.

"Bit of a layabout, is he?"

"We do not gossip in this village," said Nessie righteously. "Pass me the Bible, Jessie, and we'll hear this nice young man read to us."

It was a large Victorian Bible, illustrated with steel engravings. Feeling trapped, Cyril began to read, and, as he read, he began to experience a strange feeling of doom. His mobile phone suddenly rang, and he grabbed it out of his pocket. It was Blair, asking if there was any progress.

"Can't talk now, Mother," said Cyril. "I'll call you later." He rang off.

"You shouldn't cut your mother off like that," chided Nessie.

"How right you are." Cyril stood up and put the Bible and his cup on the table. "I'll get back to my digs and call her from there."

"We'll see you in the kirk on Sunday," said Nessie.

If I'm still alive and not dead with boredom, thought Cyril, making his escape.

"Where are we off to?" asked Dick the next morning as he climbed into the Land Rover beside Hamish.

"Do you know Sandybeach?"

"No, where's that?"

"Tiny little place up north of Scourie. Grand place for a picnic. I'll put the siren on and get Cyril chasing us."

"It's only seven in the morning," said Dick. "Think he'll be up yet?"

"Probably not. But I've phoned Jimmy. Blair's bound to ask if there's been a report of a crime, so I told him to say there was a burglary at Sandybeach."

"So what do we do if the scunner catches up with us?"

"He won't. It's so quiet up there, you can hear a car coming for miles. We'll take off for somewhere else."

The sound of the siren woke Cyril. He tumbled out of bed and dashed to the window, opened it, and hung out. He could just see the Land Rover racing out over the humpbacked bridge. He scrabbled into his clothes and phoned Blair, asking him to find out where Hamish had gone.

He had gone a mile out of Lochdubh when Blair rang. "Burglary at a place called Sandybeach."

"Where's that?"

"How should I know? Look at a map."

Cyril programmed his sat-nav and set off in pursuit. He hurtled along the one-track roads, blind to the beauty all around him. Purple heather blazed on the flanks of the soaring mountains. Rowan trees shone with bloodred berries. Above, the sky was an arch of blue. At one point, he thought he heard the sound of another driver behind him and suddenly stopped, switched off his engine, rolled down the windows, and listened. But there was nothing to be heard but the mournful call of a curlew.

Cyril crouched over the wheel and drove on.

Sutherland, the southland of the Vikings, is the most underpopulated county in the British Isles. The west coast has the most dazzling scenery. But to Cyril, it was an odd foreign landscape, alien, far from the bustle and crowds of Strathbane.

At long last, he saw a signpost pointing the way to Sandybeach.

"The end of the road," said Cyril, not knowing that, for him, it was.